KHAN

By

MICHAEL JOHNSON

Scarlet Leaf
2017

PUBLISHED BY SCARLET LEAF
Toronto, Canada

Front cover design by: Yvonne Alonso Yunca, Metro Publicity, Malaga, Spain.

BOOK 1

A TOWN IN AFRICA

CHAPTER 1
DUBAI

Micky Manning stretched his legs under the silk sheets and yawned loudly. He was not one for holding back his emotions; or his desires especially when it came to women. He was therefore smugly pleased with the sight on either side of him.

The two women could have been twins but he knew they weren't. They had come as a bonus from a grateful sponsor.

The hotel suite was not the most expensive in the Raiyat Hotel; but it came close. He had landed by Private Jet five days ago, to participate in the opening of a new golf course. He wasn't a Professional golfer but he did have a single figure handicap. No, he liked a game of golf but his Profession was much more lucrative. As a Premier League football player, he was paid more in one month than what most golfers could earn in a year.

He stretched out an arm and casually fondled the breasts of one of the girls. She moaned softly and turned over to allow him full access to her body. With his spare hand; he fondled his erection; and then cursed loudly as the telephone beside the bed started ringing.

He was tempted to ignore it but he knew who was calling so he grabbed the receiver and answered it.

'Please tell me you're out of bed Micky. I've just had a text from the Captain informing me they must depart on time due to adverse weather conditions' his manager told him.

'Adverse fucking weather conditions are you serious Manny? It hasn't rained in this bloody place for months and I don't see many clouds outside' he answered thinking it was only his manager's way of making him get to the reception in time for the limousine's departure.

'Not here in Dubai' he wanted to add 'you're a clever dick' but resisted 'the bad weather is somewhere over Africa'

Micky wasn't convinced but he relented 'I'll be down in half an hour Manny I promise'

The girl in his bed couldn't speak a word of English so she had no idea what he had just said. She did understand however his request for her to turn over on her belly so he could enter from behind.

'Just a quickie sweetheart' he told her grinning.

As promised he was in reception half an hour later.

Manny had to admire his client 'he's been humping women non-stop for the past three days and doesn't look out of breath' he thought 'Are you fit to go?' he asked.

'Too right old son' he answered in his Cockney accent 'and I left those two nice ladies a tip they won't forget' he laughed heading for the exit.

'I bet you have. You're a smug bastard' Manny mumbled under his breath.

It wasn't that he disliked his client but the man had no morals or sense of wrong doing. As one of the most sought after players in the football league he earned the equivalent of the National Debt of a small country. He would never however be stupid enough to chastise his client. After all his ten percent was nothing to sneeze about.

Micky leaned over to his Manager in the limousine as they travelled to the airport 'you are certain the hotel will keep its mouth shut aren't you Manny' he asked earnestly.

And there it was. Micky Manning was a complete arsehole but he wasn't stupid; far from it.

'I mean the *skinny bint* won't clock me, will she?'

The *skinny bint* by the way happened to be one of the top ten models in Europe and earned just as much as he did 'no Micky they will never disclose the details of their clients stay trust me'

That seemed to satisfy him so he leaned back into the leather seats and sighed contentedly. That was until the chauffeur buzzed the intercom to inform him there was a caller on the line.

'Hello darling, how are you? Yes, sweetheart. I'm looking forward to meeting up in Marbella tomorrow! Yes, I have missed you. No, I've been a good boy and didn't drink too much. Bye. See you at the Villa' he cooed seductively as he replaced the receiver.

'You have to keep them sweet Manny' he said grinning and winking at his manager who just shook his head.

Talented, rich and the bastards too good looking for his own good but you can't help liking the guy all the same he thought to himself.

Micky and Manny were the last to board the private jet transporting them to Southern Spain. There were only two other passengers; a middle-aged business man and a teenage boy both dressed in Arab Garb.

The Pilot had welcomed them aboard and explained the flight would take longer than usual due to the increased military traffic over Syria. There was also a severe weather warning over the North African States but they should be flying high enough to avoid that problem. It would however cause more turbulence than normal.

'Do we have an update on that weather front' the pilot asked his co-pilot.

'Yes Captain' he answered soberly 'it's heading due north and causing a lot of problems on the ground but we should avoid it on our route'

'Are you happy with the engineer's report' he asked checking his clip board.

'He couldn't find anything wrong with the fuel injectors' he shrugged 'but I have requested a full overhaul the minute we touch down in Malaga'

The Captain wasn't completely happy but if the engines past inspection there was nothing he could do. The Company didn't look favourably on its Pilots grounding aircraft for no reason and upsetting their very wealthy clients.

Micky was fast asleep ten minutes after taking off. Even the turbulence didn't disturb his snoring until suddenly he sat up and looked around the cabin 'did you hear that Manny' he whispered across the aisle to him.

Manny had no idea what he was talking about and just shook his head annoyed at the fact he had just dozed off.

Ten minutes later he was shaken awake 'there's something wrong with this plane Manny I know there is. The engines have been making some funny noises I'm telling you'

Manny was just about to tell his client to piss off but he too became aware of the sudden tension in the cabin. The Stewardess was walking back and forth to the cockpit trying not to look troubled.

Then it happened. The port engine cut out making the plane bank sharply to the right. It lost altitude.   The Stewardess for all her experience couldn't stop herself crashing into the bulkhead and groaning in pain of the broken arm.   The Captain told everyone to fasten their seat belts and assume the crash position. They were going down.

CHAPTER 2
AN AFRICAN STATE

Mohammed Khan stood up from his position and shook the sand from his clothing. The sand storm had finally passed by, leaving the landscape swept clean.

'At least it stopped the shelling' he thought gazing into the distance where the government troops where entrenched.

He un-wrapped the plastic bag protecting his weapon and began to break it down into parts. It would all need to be checked and oiled before re-assembly. He checked the Scope. It was clear. He fondled the Barrett M96 lovingly. It was a beautiful weapon and no mistake. How the rebel army had acquired them was a mystery but something you never asked about.

Mohammed was a believer in the rebel cause but he had not lived in his homeland for many years. His parents had taken him to America when he was just a child. He had visited the village of his birth many times however and considered it just as much his home as New York. That village was now in government hands. The people he considered family where all dead. Likely, he would also be killed soon. The cease fires had come and gone with regular monotony. The United Nations were seemingly unable or unwilling to police them. They were expendable. A forgotten conflict only fit for the occasional mention on CNN or FOX.

Mohammed became aware of a droning sound in the distance. He instinctively took cover believing the opposing forces had taken the opportunity to launch an air-strike despite the fact the area was a no-fly zone. There was a landing strip nearby once used by the UN as a staging post for their Relief Operation. It would be wishful thinking to believe that it would be again; at least anytime soon, despite the fact his people were starving to death.

Mohammed frowned and searched the skies. He could recognise a military jet by the sound of its engines but this wasn't like anything he had heard before. He saw the trail of smoke well before the small private jet came into view. It banked and lost altitude. It suddenly dawned on him it was making an emergency landing on the air strip.

Mohammed grabbed his radio and contacted the command post in the town behind him. Without waiting for orders, he jumped down from his concealed position and waved to his men to follow him. He could now make out the British markings on the tail. If these were European's, he wanted to know why they had been made an emergency landing in such a remote area. The men, guarding the airfield where uneducated and knew no other language but their own. They may shoot first and ask questions later!

CRASH LANDING

Captain Carrington resisted the temptation to curse. He should have insisted on a complete engine over haul but now was not the time to beat him-self up. The Port engine had died without warning making them lose altitude. It couldn't have happened at a worse time. A few thousand feet below the weather front had obliterated the landscape. They were at the edge of the storms fury but the sand particles had never the less bombarded them. It was only a matter of time before the starboard engine began to protest at the battering. They had no option but to try and land the plane but the desert stretched for thousands of miles in every direction. It was by pure chance the co-pilot saw the old landing strip in the distance. It took all their experience to coax the small jet towards the flat strip of land in the distance as the instruments began to fail one by one.

The co-pilot managed to glance out of the cockpit window for a second. What he saw made him even more worried than the possibility of crash landing. Down below military vehicles were standing in a neat line. At the front a row of Tanks pointed their barrels at the small town in the distance.

'Holy shit what are we getting ourselves into' he groaned.

The remaining engine cut out as the wheels touched down. Without reverse power the jet continued to career down the bumpy runway. It ran out of tarmac and crashed through a perimeter fence. The landing gear buckled but held long enough for the plane to come to a complete stop. The jet crashed onto the sandy earth below. It had the benefit of extinguishing the fire that was about to erupt.

Within a few minutes the crew and passengers where spilling out of the wreckage.

They should have taken more notice of the heavily armed men in Arab clothing surrounding them before congratulating themselves on a miracle escape.

Micky couldn't believe they had survived. He slapped the captain on the back and hugged his manager 'that was fucking awesome Manny. Wait till the frigging Press get a load of this I'm going to be bloody famous mate I'm telling you'

'I should hold off the press conference if I was you mate' Manny said pointing to a group of men approaching them.

'Ah! They are just locals coming to say hello' he said dismissing the fact they were all armed to the teeth 'probably want my frigging autograph when they realise who I am' he said striding off to meet them.

The Arab men stood still not quite sure what to do. They had been told to wait for a local Commander to join them and take charge.

Micky was in no mood to wait around however 'Hey you' he shouted pointing at one of them 'where's the nearest telephone mate I need to make a call'

No response.

'Oh, *shit* they don't speak English' he said annoyed at such a thing then mimicking a telephone 'where...is...your....tel..e...phone' he spelt out.

No response.

'Frigging dumb cloth heads' he shouted annoyed and trying to push through the line of men.

No response.

'Look mate. Get the hell out of the way before I....'

The rifle butt slammed into his groin.

The pain took a split second to register. Micky sank to his knees in pain and vomited.

Manny rushed over and helped his client away from the grinning men.

'*Tel...e...phone*' one of them mimicked.

Mohammed arrived as the injured Micky was led away. He quickly gave orders to the men surrounding the plane who recognised one of their more educated brethren.

He approached the small group of men and the one woman. She was clearly in pain and probably the Stewardess.

The Pilot and Co-Pilot were easily recognisable but he would talk to them later. Two were European. Two were Arabs. He would question them all eventually but first he needed to examine the aircraft especially the flight manifest.

He waited and as expected the Captain approached him 'are you in charge here' he asked politely.

The New York accent would come as a shock 'yes Captain I am. My name is Mohammed Khan. What is your name?'

'My apologies, my name is Captain John Carrington and this is my Co-pilot Jim Steele. We had to make an emergency landing as you can see' he said pointing to the wreckage 'I would be grateful if you could contact our people to let them know we are alive' he sighed.

The relief at meeting a possible friend was obvious.

'I will certainly do that I assure you' he replied 'but why don't we get your cabin crew to a doctor. She looks in pain.' he said.

He turned around and gave orders to two men close by.

'Thank you Mister Khan. That is most kind of you. I will go with her'

'She will be quite safe' he replied ignoring the request out of hand 'who are your passengers'

The Captain was so relieved at being helped by a possible friend he told him everything he knew about the four men 'the older Arab gentleman is a very wealthy business man from Dubai on his way to procure a large contract in Spain. The young Arab man is related to the Royal Household and was on his way to meet his Uncle. The two Englishmen are involved in Football. By all accounts the young one is a well-known football player in their country'

It was all designed to import the importance of his passengers so they would be well treated and allowed to contact their head office in London for help.

Mohammed smiled in satisfaction.

He turned again to the guards and gave them orders.

'You and your Co-Pilot will accompany these men. The passengers will be taken to a secure location. Please do not give them any reason to hurt you Captain. They are hungry and will not tolerate *any* escape attempt' he said coldly.

The Captain took a step back angry at himself for being so open about his passengers. He now realised the man he was talking to was potentially no friend.

CHAPTER 3

MINISTRY OF DEFENCE LONDON

The MI6 Director waited patiently in the ante-room.

The file on his lap was wrapped in red tape and marked Confidential.

The intercom on the desk of the Personal Secretary opposite began humming.

She smiled at the MI6 Director 'the Minister is ready for you Sir Henry' she informed him politely.

He nodded and entered the oak panelled room.

'Please take a seat Sir Henry I'll be with you in a moment' the Minister advised; waving to a chair his desk.

The Director did so. He was a seasoned Civil Servant and knew the protocol for such meetings off by heart. He would not talk until the man opposite began the conversation.

The Minister closed the file on his desk and tossed it to one side 'my American counterpart in Washington has been on the telephone; asking if we require their services in freeing the *hostages* Sir Henry. I thanked him and suggested everything was in hand; but of course, I would keep them well briefed. What I didn't say was that I had no idea what he was talking about which is why I called you. I assume that file is for me; that is if MI6 actually know what is happening in North Africa!'

It was said politely but the barb was not lost on the Director.

'My apologies Minister but the seriousness of the situation only became apparent after the call from Langley'

The Minister was tempted to continue the veiled dressing down but he knew he would come out a looser in the long run.

'Tell me what you know Sir Henry. I understand the Americans were contacted by one of their own.' he asked.

'If you mean an American citizen then yes, it's true. However; what you may not know is the man was once a CIA Operative'

The Minister didn't know and raised his eyebrows at the news.

The MI6 Director continued 'Michael Khan; now known as Mohammed Khan moved to New York with his parents when he was only five. His father still lives in Manhattan but his mother passed away when he was ten. Michael Khan made frequent visits to his old home with his father before joining the Marine Corps as a Cadet. By all accounts he was top of his class in almost everything and quickly rose in the ranks. The CIA recruited him by dangling the bait of frequent visits to Africa. It was about this time the Elders of the tribe where asking for autonomy from the central government. The timing couldn't have been worse as we well knew so soon after The Arab Spring. Khan was asked to contact the newly formed Council to suggest just that but he couldn't persuade them to hold off their demands'

The Minister nodded as he remembered what happened next 'you have to hand it to the newly formed government. They conned us for months with promises of mediation and constructive talks before blowing the hell out of that first village. The UN finally got involved only after the second one was being flattened. The no-fly zone grounded their bombers but not the tanks on the ground. Unfortunately, it also meant we couldn't supply aide to the only airfield in the region capable of landing cargo planes'

The MI6 Director nodded in agreement.

He was going to add 'it also meant the Americans couldn't supply weapons after the town was surrounded' but decided to keep that information to himself.

'Are the hostages in any danger? I mean of being killed that is' the Minister asked.

'My sources in the area say no; at least not from their captors'

'I don't understand Sir Henry who else could harm them?'

'It's all in my Report Minister' he replied nodding to the file on his desk 'but maybe I should give you an update before your meeting with the PM later'

The Minister was about to ask a stupid question; this man knew everything that was going on; it was his job after all!

'I will not explain the political and cultural differences that led to these people asking for Autonomy from the central government as I'm sure you already know all that. They are not considered terrorists by any means; in fact, just the opposite which is why the West wanted to provide aide. One of the problems has also been; the Tribe as they like to call themselves are spread out over a wide area. In fact, most them live across the border where they do enjoy a measure of autonomy'

'I understand there was a mass exodus just before the town was surrounded'

'That's true Minister. But there are still many civilians; women and children among them'

'And quite probably starving to death!' the Minister added angrily.

'The UN have been pushing for a cease fire for months. The first aid convoy should have arrived last week'

'But was mysteriously attacked by so called Militants' the Minister added even more angrily.

'Quite so, which is why they have not sanctioned another convoy. I have to say that jet couldn't have landed in a worse place and at the *wrong time*'

The Minister sat up in his chair 'OK why the *wrong time*?'

'We have just received the latest recognisance photos' he said passing over some Arial photographs 'it seems the Government forces have been moving Troops and Tanks during the recent storm'

The Minister studied the photographs and looked up 'my god they are within spitting distance of that town!'

'That is so Minister and if my intel is correct; they will be launching an attack at o-six hundred tomorrow morning local time'

'Jesus Christ, it will be a massacre!'

The Minister sat back and scratched his head thoughtfully. He had been hoping the situation could have been resolved by some quiet negotiations and bribes if necessary but that idea was now out of the window. If the hostages got caught up in a fire fight they wouldn't stand a chance. The Media would have a birthday with the blame game. The PM wasn't that popular now and this would play into the Oppositions stance on non-intervention.

'We have to get those people out Sir Henry. Any ideas?'

'If you are considering some kind of rescue operation with our Special Forces I would strongly advise against it. Apart from the lack of time the Elders of the tribe would consider it a betrayal. We could turn a non-militant tribe into just the opposite. Besides there is no indication they are at risk from the local people. Like I said just the opposite'

'So why can't we just ask for them to be returned' he asked.

'We can and we will but this Mohammed Khan is no fool. By now he will have split the crew and passengers up and into various locations. He will be in no hurry to arrange safe conduct even if the opposing forces are interested in agreeing to one. I assume the PM will be asking our Ambassador to call on the President but we both know how long that meeting can be delayed. By the time they meet that town will be wiped off the map'

The Minister was now fidgeting in his chair and scratching his head even more.

This could turn into a political nightmare and they were powerless to intervene.

'Unfortunately, I have to agree with your assessment Sir Henry. Their President will deny any knowledge of the downed jet. Even when they do they can pretend their assault on the town was some sort of rescue mission. The odds of these people coming out alive are zero!'

'There is one other thing you need to tell the PM; Minister!' the MI6 Director added cautiously.

'Oh, shit this thing can't get any worse, can it?' he moaned.

'We now have the passenger list from Dubai. We know about the football player and his manager and about the Saudi Prince but the fourth passenger was not known to us until we received his passport details' he stated handing over a separate file marked Eyes Only.

The Minister opened it and read the information.

It just got very worse indeed.

He was just about to comment when the door burst open 'I think you should watch the news Minister' the secrctary advised switching on a screen mounted on the wall.

BBC NEWS ITEM.......... the ticker tape at the bottom of the screen ran a constant message…. *Premier League Football Player Micky Manning held hostage in Africa…. Premier League Football Player Micky Manning…………* it continued to say.

The Minister made an audible groan at what he was reading on the screen. He was about to make a comment when suddenly the news presenter came on live. She paused for dramatic effect before reading the auto cue.

Earlier today at approximately 8.15 GMT Flight BX 707 - a Privately chartered on route from Dubai to Southern Spain was forced to make an emergency landing somewhere in Northern Africa. We can now confirm that Premier League football player Micky Manning and his Manager where passengers aboard the flight. It is understood both men are safe and well but are hostages of the breakaway State seeking Independence from the central government.

The female news reader turned to her left '*Professor McCarthy is a senior lecturer on Middle East and African politics*'……she announced…… '*Professor what is your assessment of the situation in ……….!!!*'

'Oh, turn the bloody sound down' the Minister growled at his secretary 'last thing I need right now is advice from some loony Professor!'

The MI6 Director made no comment but his mind was assessing what had just happened.

The secretary returned to her desk. The red dials on her telephone where lighting up one by one. She answered them all politely and efficiently promising each caller the Minister would call back as soon as possible. The one from the PM she put through immediately.

After the Minister, had taken the call and replaced the receiver, he looked at the MI6 Director 'if you have any ideas; I would like to hear them'

The MI6 Director collected his thoughts before answering 'this is a smart move by Mohammed Khan. He is letting the world know he has the crew and the passengers. My guess is; he will make a video to show the world they are safe and well. If I was him; I would separate them into small groups and mould each one to my way of thinking'

'What good would that do? Is he capable of such interrogation techniques?'

'If you read his file Minister he is more than capable trust me. If I am right; the first video will feature the Air Stewardess. I understand she has a broken arm. She is also a French National'

'The French get very emotional when one of their own is in trouble. Especially if its female and good looking'

'Quite so Minister!'

CHAPTER 4

A TOWN IN NORTHERN AFRICA

Mohammed Khan jumped aboard a waiting jeep which sped off down the bumpy road in a cloud of dust. Only a week ago, such a thing would have been unthinkable. One of the carefully camouflaged tanks just over a mile away could have been tempted to fire a few shells at such an easy target.

The jeep came to a halt in front of a sign saying *Hospital.* It was the only indication of what the building had previously been used for. Now it was just a shell. The upper floors where pock marked with holes. None of the windows had glass in them. Ripped and shredded curtains fluttered occasionally as the light breeze caught them.

TWO HOURS EARLIER

Claudia Deveraux had arrived at the hospital. She was still in a state of shock from surviving the plane crash albeit with a broken arm which was now causing her severe discomfort. She had been shocked at the devastation in the small town. Looking up at the hospital made her want to cry at the brutality of it all.

She was escorted down to the basement which was now the only safe place to house the wounded and the infirm. As the double doors swung shut behind her she found herself rooted to the spot unable to move.

Down both sides of the long corridor men, women and children lay on make shift beds, mattresses or just the floor. Saline drips administered medicine to the neediest but the moans and anguished cries from many others bore reference to the lack of pain killers and antibiotics.

A man in a white smock approached and introduced himself as a doctor *'actually I was just a medical student but as all the real Doctors are dead that puts me in charge'* he said resignedly in French.

It took a few seconds for her to realise he was speaking in her native language. The man was barely into his twenties and yet had taken on such a responsibility.

Claudia began to sob shamelessly as the realisation of her predicament was brought home to her.

Mohammed entered the only private cubicle in the make shift ward; an old storeroom.

The air stewardess was sitting in a wicker chair trying desperately not to fall asleep. The doctor had provided an update on her condition 'I had to reset the bone before strapping the arm. That woman is stronger than she looks. We have no pain killers left Mohammed!' he stated a matter of fact.

He nodded in understanding and approached the woman.

'Hello Claudia! How are you feeling?' he asked kindly.

Claudia took a deep breath and sat up intent of not letting her Captain down by falling to pieces and embarrassing the Company *'I am well thankyou sir. The Doctor has re-set the arm the best he could; under the circumstances'* she stated in French.

'I am pleased to hear that but is it possible we speak in English. My French has always been a little rusty'

'I think your French is better than you think sir' she answered.

'Thank you, Claudia. My name in case you missed it at the crash site is Mohammed Khan but I was known as Michael when I lived in New York with my parents'

'Are your parents still alive' she asked suddenly getting interested in the man's history.

She also realised that under the Arab clothing there was a most handsome face.

'My father still lives in Manhattan but my mother passed away when I was young' he shrugged.

'I'm sorry to hear that. How did you come to be here?'

Mohammed sat crossed legged on the floor and adjusted his clothing. He pulled off the head scarf he was wearing and ruffled his straggly hair attempting to shake the sand away. It was all designed to put the stewardess at ease and believe she was in charge; but time was short.

'I have been travelling back and forth to America ever since I was a young man. My father wanted me to be aware of the family history. In time, I came to look upon these people as my own. When I left the American Marine Corps, I came here to live and fell in love with a local woman. We married and had a child'

'That's a wonderful story; are they here with you?' she asked already forgetting the destruction on the streets above.

'They are all **dead** Claudia!' he stated frankly.

Claudia gulped and tried to hold back the cry of anguish. Her heart went out to the handsome man sitting cross-legged in front of her 'I'm so sorry Mohammed'

Mohammed let the enormity of his story sink in before continuing 'it is in the past Claudia. The Koran teaches us many things and is of great comfort in desperate times:

'God does not forbid you from being good to those who have not fought you in the religion or driven you from your home, or being just towards them. God loves those who are just'
(Suret al-Mumtahana)

'You do not hate the people who killed your family?' she asked astonished.

'They are miss-guided and have lost their way Claudia. With Allah's help we will one day overcome their fears and distrust'

'I do not think I would be so forgiving Mohammed. I would also like to tell you I am sorry'

Mohammed frowned at the statement 'I do not understand Claudia. What are you sorry for?'

'I am sorry for the way I think of Muslims. You must know what has happened in my country over the past few years. Many of my countrymen including myself consider all people of your religion to be evil. I can now see I have been naive and bigoted'

Mohammed was taken aback by the statement but kept his composure. He had a job to do and this young woman was key to his plans. Time was of the essence. In exactly six hours' time the government forces would begin their attack on the town.

It was time to ask the question.

'Claudia, I want to be honest with you about our situation here. We are cut off from our people across the border. We have no food or clean water. Just a mile away the government army is poised to attack this town. We will be fighting Challenger Tanks bought from the British Government with rocket propelled grenades and small arms. We will stand our ground and be slaughtered in the process'

'But surely you can surrender? What about the women and children?' she cried.

'They will be considered a casualty of war. I know the General in command of their elite troops. He is not a man to show mercy or leave anyone alive to answer awkward questions!'

Something suddenly dawned on her 'what about the passengers and crew of our jet. Surely they will not kill us as well'

'I'm afraid Claudia you will be the greatest *awkward question of them all*'

IN ANOTHER PART OF TOWN

Micky Manning was pacing the room continuously kicking any object that wasn't tied down and that was most things.

Manny had long since given up trying to calm his client down.

In truth, he was very worried.

They had been led through the town by armed guards who had mysteriously disappeared as soon as they were settled in a hotel room.

The hotel room still had a bed and most of its fittings intact. Not beneficial as there was no running water. The toilet was already giving off a strong odour.

Manny had been surprised the hotel was still intact given the destruction in the town itself. They had been given a bottle of water with hand signals to say it should be drank sparingly. Micky had ignored them and drank the water in one go. They were now beginning to realise that was a bad mistake.

Micky was getting more agitated by the hour. He had already come up with a scheme to escape.

'This is not some frigging World War Two Movie Micky. There are real men out there with real weapons who won't hesitate to shoot you on sight' he told him getting angry.

'But we've got to do something Manny the *skinny bint* is expecting me in Marbella this time tomorrow'

Manny could only gape at his client's inability to understand their predicament.

The trouble was; he wasn't himself. There were no guards in the corridor or anywhere else for that matter. He had even wondered down to the lobby to have a look around. No one had bothered him. It was all a bit of a mystery.

He heard a vehicle come to a halt outside and went to the balcony to see what was happening.

Down below the man at the airport who called himself Mohammed got out of a jeep and went around to the other door to help his passenger.

It was the air stewardess.

'Hey Micky come and look at this' he beckoned.

Micky watched as the stewardess was escorted into the building 'looks like she's had the arm sorted. Is it my imagination or do they look pretty pally together?'

'She certainly doesn't look under any duress; as they say in the movies' Manny answered.

A few minutes later a knock came at the door and Mohammed entered 'I trust you are being taken care of gentlemen' he asked politely.

Micky was just about to go into one of his rants but Manny stopped him 'what's going to happen to us' he asked bluntly.

Mohammed raised his hands in the air mimicking he had no idea.

'It all depends on what your governments decide to do. I am here to help but I can only do so much'

'That's a load of bollocks Manny and you know it. If he wanted to help; then all he has to do is set us all free'

'But you are free to leave any time Mister Manning; although I wouldn't advise it *just* yet' Mohammed answered still smiling.

'Ok Mohammed I'll bite. Why shouldn't we leave now?' Manny asked.

'Because in all likely hood you would never reach the enemies position before being shot. Many times, I would think!'

The two Englishmen looked at each other not knowing what to say.

Mohammed was still smiling both outwardly and inwardly. He had placed a conundrum in the minds of the two men. It was time to offer a solution.

'Maybe I should explain our position. This town is surrounded by government troops who should be abiding by the UN Ceasefire Resolution. They are not. In fact, they are about to do the exact opposite. During the sand storm that was responsible for downing your private jet; the General in command has been moving significant amounts of artillery and men. In less than six hours he will order his Tanks to open fire on the town. After that his well-armed and highly trained Elite Commandoes will storm into the town. They will not distinguish between fighter or civilian, woman or child. They have orders to eradicate all trace of our culture and heritage.

We will stand and fight and almost certainly die but that is the Will of Allah is it not'

The two men had gone deathly white listening to what was about to happen. Micky ran to the sink and retched into the bowl.

'You said we could help to avoid all this. What do you need from us?'

'Join me on the balcony' Mohammed suggested 'while your friend recovers from the shock'

Out on the balcony he waved his arm in a wide arc 'this was once a prosperous and happy town. All that we asked was to be free to make our own decisions. It is a common enough request in many parts of the world. The Basques in Northern Spain for example. Even in your country Scotland wishes independence. To deny such a request only serves to alienate the local population and make them more militant. We tried to avoid such a scenario by trusting in the United Nations. We were wrong in doing so but by then the war of attrition had already started. I am sure by now you realise I was not raised in this country. My father emigrated to America when I was a young boy. My father still lives in New York. I have many contacts there but they can only do so much' he ended.

Micky had been listening to the conversation 'so you're keeping us here so the Yanks can send a few tanks to help out' he asked.

'A few tanks as you put it will do no good against a well-trained and resourceful enemy. No Mister Manning what we need are more basic items. Things you would take for granted. One meal a day. Clean water to drink and enough to wash our clothes in. Medical supplies to relieve the suffering of those injured or just ill. A few days in the open without fear of being shot by a sniper. The freedom to worship in our own way. To rebuild our homes so the families can join their loved ones and be safe. Is this too much to ask Mr Manning?'

Micky was now feeling about two inches high. He had become used to the rich and famous life style afforded a Premier League football player; but he hadn't forgotten his roots.

Micky Manning was the product of an English mother and an Irish Father. Living in the East End of London he quickly learned life wasn't always easy and you needed to look after yourself. He managed to struggle through his exams but by then it was obvious where his talents lay. He could control and kick a football like no other. Two weeks after leaving school he was enrolled into a local Football Academy. A year later he was playing centre forward for the first team. The rest as they say is history.

Micky moved on to the balcony and for the first time looked at the devastation in the old town. Once proud buildings had been reduced to no more than a shell. Shop fronts which had only months ago, bustled with activity selling local produce were now empty and abandoned. An old woman hurried across the street with a bundle in her arms, probably the only possession she had left.

It was a far cry from the happy and prosperous streets of London.

He turned to Mohammed 'if we can't leave this place before they start the attack are you saying we are as good as dead?'

Mohammed shrugged and raised his hands again 'we are all in the hands of Allah or whatever God you worship' he replied looking more at Manny who suddenly made the sign of the cross.

Mohammed had guessed correctly.

Being from an Irish background the odds where Manny had been brought up a Catholic. He suspected the football player had no such religious upbringing so another approach was needed.

'I understand you are a famous football player Mr. Manning. Do you also play for your country in this sport? Forgive my ignorance but in America football means a different thing although I suspect they do not have the same life style as your own'

Micky just laughed 'come on mate I've seen those cheerleaders waving their pompoms about. Those football players have got it made and don't tell me they're not well paid'

'That is true Mr. Manning very true' Mohammed agreed shrugging 'they may not admit it but they would still like to have honour titles. I am a great admirer of your Royal Family'

Micky was now frowning at the sudden change in the conversation. He wasn't quite sure what the Arab was getting at.

Mohammed waited a few moments before continuing 'football players like yourself are proud to play for their country. It is only right they should be rewarded by your Queen. I understand they are called knighthoods. We do not have anything like this in America as you probably know'

Micky had never considered this little perk sometime in the future; but *Sir* Micky was now firmly planted in his mind 'If that dozy prat Linaker can get one, I'm dam sure I can' he decided.

Mohammed waited again to let the idea sink in 'the only problem with these titles is you have to be near retirement I understand. That or do something extraordinary'

Micky was hooked.

Mohammed walked to the door to leave 'we have very little food and water but I will make sure you have enough for your needs. I must go. We are about to make a video with your stewardess Miss Deveraux a very charming and sensitive young woman by the way. She is French as you may well know. A language I speak very badly I'm afraid'

Manny couldn't resist it 'what kind of video? Not one of those Terrorist demands we see on TV, is it?'

'I would have thought by now you had realised we are a peaceful people who would never condone violence or atrocities you see in other countries Mister Manning. Miss

Deveraux is making this video of her own free will, but please do not take my word for it. You are welcome to observe!'

THE HOTEL BASEMENT

The basement was in fact the communications and command centre. The Elders would meet to discuss strategy and issue commands. It was also the last remaining way to contact the world outside.

When the three men entered, Claudia was sitting on a stool facing a mounted camera. There was just a plain blue screen behind her.

The opposing Government General in Command knew where this communication centre was located; and had deliberately avoided targeting the building; thinking it would make a good command centre for himself when he *cleared* the town.

Mohammed nodded to the engineer who had been instructed to wait for them.

He then pulled up another stool and sat behind the camera.

He made eye contact with the stewardess and smiled warmly. She responded by mirroring the smile. Claudia was already falling a little in love with the good-looking Arab with so much weight on his shoulders.

'Please state your name and occupation for the camera' he asked.

She did so.

'Are you here of your own free will'

She answered 'yes'

'This is the only thing I will ask you to do. From now on all your words must be your own'

Claudia nodded in understanding and smiled again. By the time, she finished; tears were rolling down her cheeks and she was sobbing uncontrollably. She had graphically detailed the suffering of the people and the lack of basic items the rest of the world took for granted. She had admired their integrity and honour under such provocation and brutality from the Government forces but it was her conviction at the end which even surprised Mohammed.

'I have been told the town will be attacked in a few hours. The men here have no way to repulse such an onslaught and have already said their goodbyes to their loved ones; the ones who have refused to abandon them that is. We are not prisoners and may leave at any time. As the town is surrounded it would be quite likely we would be shot on sight. However, I must tell you I will stay here and suffer the same fate as these proud people. I will not be leaving. I beg the people of France to demand the United Nations stop this atrocity or they will have blood on their hands!'

The two men in the background started clapping. Even Mohammed was staggered at such an emotional response.

'Thankyou Claudia' he said helping her from the stool.

She staggered slightly and he caught her in his arms. Claudia couldn't help herself and hugged him close ignoring the aroma of days sitting in a ditch.

He handed her over to a guard 'make sure she is safe and has as much food and water as we can spare' he ordered. He needed to focus and she was a distraction. He also needed to show the two men he had integrity and would not take advantage of her.

'The video will be sent to the French News Corporations just as soon as it is edited. I am not sure if it will do any good. It will be in French of course so it will only really make an impact in that country'

'Why don't you make one in English then' Micky asked

'You are the only two Englishmen here apart from the planes Captain and Co-Pilot of course but I suspect that making an appeal to their government for help would not be acceptable to them. They are both ex RAF pilots and would not consider it. In the event of an attack you must come down to this basement by the way. It may be the only safe place' he finished before suggesting they return to their rooms.

Mohammed waited until the two Englishmen had departed then joined the technician in the control room 'do you have all the footage you need for the backdrop' he asked.

'Yes, Mohammed I filmed the hospital ward earlier. I have more than enough homes being blown away trust me'

'Good.   I am confident the English footballer player will also make the same appeal. Maybe not as good as the woman though'

'She did sound very sincere I agree. I think she likes you Mohammed' he said grinning.

'I was impressed I have to admit; but now is not the time for flirtation' he replied.

'We may all be dead this time tomorrow Mohammed. I think there is no better time for flirtation; especially with one so beautiful' he came back.

He smiled at the technician's attitude. It was the same with all his people. They had resigned themselves to their fate; whatever that may be.

'There is one more thing I have to do before interviewing the two Arabs.   The younger one is a family member of the Royal Family.   Probably well connected but not enough as to warrant direct intervention from the Saudi Government. They have not been inclined to take sides in the past and I see no reason for them to do so now. The other Arab is a mystery though'

'I thought he was just a business man on a trip to purchase property or some kind of commercial development in Spain'

'That's what the Captain told me but I sensed there was something he was keeping back'

'We have no way of checking his credentials Mohammed'

'You haven't but I may have a way. It is a long time since I saw her but I believe she is now working for the CIA in Langley. I will use her private e mail address if it's still active. From then on its up to her'

The technician had the sense not to ask who *her* was.

CHAPTER 5
USA – CIA HEADQUARTERS

Katherine Carter was about to finish work for the day when her cell phone pinged. She didn't recognise the number and was about to delete it as another nuisance call when she realised the sender was not from the USA. In fact, she wasn't sure exactly where it had come from accept it was from possibly North Africa.

Her curiosity got the better of her and she opened the file and took an intake of breath as she recognised the sender 'Michael Khan!'

YEARS EARLIER

The training had been tough with more than one Agent admitting defeat and quitting the course. The instructors knew their business and could spot a failure before he or she admitted it to themselves. They could however also spot the ones who had potential to go all the way. Michael Khan and Katherine Carter were in this category excelling at everything that was put in front of them. They were also both very good looking with athletic figures. It was only a matter of time before the obvious attraction between them was too much to control. They became lovers the minute the course ended. It was to last many months before they both agreed it wasn't going to work. They were both dedicated to their careers. The long separations also didn't help. Khan eventually disappeared to North Africa for good. She was happy when she learned of his marriage and impending family. She was distraught when she learned they had all been killed in the village where they lived.

Katherine opened the file and read the request. It was simple enough. Who is this person?

She downloaded the attachment and transferred it to her work screen. From now on everything she did would be monitored. The name didn't register any alarm bells until possible aliases were requested. By the time the Facial Recognition programme had confirmed who the Arab was Katherine knew she was in trouble. Before she had time to transfer the information two CIA Special Agents came through the door to her office and *advised* her the CIA Station Head of Control would like to have a word with her.

She was tempted to hit the send button first knowing it could possibly end her career. She didn't.

The Station Head had already taken advice from further up the chain of command. What she was told to do surprised even her.

'Please come in Katherine and take a seat' she told a nervous agent 'I think there is something you need to tell me'

'I'm sorry Mam I had no idea who the Arab was'

'Of course, you didn't otherwise you would have come to me straight away. Your security rating was only increased last week otherwise you would never have been allowed to access the file. But you are and you did so that's done with. The question is why!'

Katherine had been with the agency long enough to know that by now her private e mails were being examined 'the request came from.......' she didn't finish the sentence before the Section Head stopped her.

'Please do not tell me where it came from. The less I know the better at this stage. The question is; are you going to reply. Now! What you do or who you contact via your private e mails is nothing to do with the Agency. Do you understand?'

Katherine was confused for a moment then just nodded. Something was going on but she had the sense not to enquire further 'thankyou mam. I think my shift has finished. Time for me to go home'

'That's it then. Goodnight Miss Carter'

The Section Head waited until the Agent was well out of the office before picking up the phone 'I assume you *are* going to explain what's going on'

'This request can only have come from Michael Khan in North Africa' she was told.

'You mean the same place that Private Jet crash landed. Are you saying he was a passenger' she asked sitting upright for the answer.

'It looks like it. We had no idea where the Arab had disappeared to and the British MI6 were not very forthcoming. They've been keeping his whereabouts secret even from us'

'But why was he travelling on his own without security?'

'We can speculate but it would only be that. Have you suggested the agent respond to the request for information'?

'I made no such suggestion obviously; but I would think your Mister Khan is going to be very pleased to learn who this Arab is'

There was a pause at the end of the line then the CIA Director came back on 'I suggest you turn on your monitor and tune in to the French News Agencies' he said before clicking off.

The Section Head did.

The face of Claudia Deveraux was displayed on the screen.

LONDON

The Minister returned to his office frustrated and a little annoyed with the decision taken by the Prime Minister and his advisors. There was to be no direct intervention such as a rescue mission. Defence contracts were in the balance. The UN has everything under control. We cannot be seen interfering in internal problems even if it did mean the annihilation of a whole community. Let the Diplomats work it out. The excuses mounted by the minute.

He was annoyed but not surprised. Ever since the Gulf War the West and even America had a policy of non-intervention; at least on the ground. They would prefer to be bombed the baddies from the air instead.

But this was different. He knew the history of these people and felt they should have been supported better in their efforts for *independence*; a word every English Minister and Member of Parliament blanched at when it was mentioned in public.

The MI6 Director had warned them this story was far from over.

'We cannot send in a Special Forces extraction team for a football player and his manager. The Pilot and Co-Pilot are ex RAF and will know the score. We have no confirmation the Government troops are going to attack the town. They insist they're only doing routine military exercises in line with the UN Resolution. I for one am not going to upset the delicate balance we have now. I feel sorry for the hostages and will do everything *diplomatically* I can' spouted the new Overseas Defence Secretary.

There was nothing else to say after that.

His Personal Secretary entered and again switched on the wall mounted TV screen 'I think you should see this Minister' she said as she left the room and closing the door.

The channel was Sky News but the story was being transmitted from a TV Station in France. It was in French of course so the translation was being shown on the bottom of the screen. The Minister spoke fluent French so he turned up the volume. The screen showed an attractive young woman dressed in an air stewardess uniform. One arm was tucked inside the jacket heavily bandaged. She had obviously cleaned her face but there was no make-up. Her eyes had dark rings around them probably due to the strain of her captivity or the pain from the broken arm it was difficult to tell.   The Minister was expecting ransom requests or threats of retaliation if their *demands* were not met. He was not expecting the intense and heart felt appeal about to unfold. Any idea she had been coerced or was under duress was quickly dispelled.

She began her appeal:

The Video:

.......My name is Claudia Deveraux and I am speaking to you from..........

The Minister like everyone else watching the broadcast was soon overcome with emotion. Behind the young woman there were scenes of devastation. Bodies of men, women and children were graphically displayed; laying where they had died in the streets. The patients in the hospital where she had received treatment were shown in all its squalor.

'Dam but that Khan is good' the Minister said to himself.

Within one hour the video went viral.

It was then that the second appeal appeared.

CHAPTER 6

THE TOWN

Captain Carrington and his co-pilot Jim Steele had noted the lack of guards around their accommodation; if that's what you would call a derelict house with two old mattresses and a table.

'What the hell is going on Captain. Are we prisoners or not' Steele asked.

'Beats me Jim. That guy who brought us that bottle of water just left. We could probably walk out of here and it seems no one would stop us'

'We both know that's not going to happen until we know Claudia and the passengers are safe. What's happening do you think'

'We had an up-date on the conflict here before we took off. The UN consider the situation under control and a diplomatic end was in sight. It didn't mention this town is under siege and the occupants are starving to death. There's a no-fly zone corridor stretching from the border and two hundred miles to the west but my understanding is; there's no military aircraft patrolling the area on a regular basis'

'They have all their resources tied up in Syria and Iraq that's why. Wasn't there supposed to be another Carrier Fleet entering the Med?'

'A joint French and British exercise if I remember rightly which is why our flightpath needed to be changed as you know'

'Sod this for a lark' the Captain growled 'let's take a walk and find out what's happening'

The two pilots had walked only a few yards when a jeep skidded to halt in front of them.

Mohammed jumped out 'Captain Carrington please accept my apologies for not visiting you earlier but things have been quite hectic. Please jump in and I will take you to more appropriate lodgings' he said opening the door to the jeep.

'Where are my passengers and stewardess Mr. Khan' he demanded angrily.

'They are safe and well I assure you Captain but come and see for yourself. It is a good thing I came when I did. Were you going for a walk? Not advisable in this full moon. The snipers hidden in the dunes out there may decide to take a pot shot; as you English might say'

The two men looked towards the end of the rubble strewn street. It was a full moon but still pitch black beyond the end of the street.

'Very good Mr. Khan let's go' the Captain decided.

Mohammed drove slowly as though craters or land mines were around every corner. He needed time to interrogate the two Pilots while they were off guard and concentrating on the road ahead.

'Only a few weeks ago, this was a vibrant and happy town Captain. Crime was almost non-existent. You do not steal from your friends or family and most of the people were just that' he said shrugging 'Disputes where settled between families or if a serious crime was committed the Elders would pass judgement'

'You seem to be living in a world of your own Khan but that's not always a good thing'

'Oh, don't get me wrong Captain. Our young people are well educated but not by Western standards I think. They learn computer skills and have access to the world-wide web. At least they used to' he said shaking his head at the devastation all around them.

'I was led to believe the situation here had stabilised'

'The government propaganda machine is very effective is it not' Mohammed replied as he stopped the jeep in front of a burnt-out building 'this was once our most prestigious University. It was full of students when the bombs hit it. I will not describe the horror of pulling dead children from the ruins but the cries of the mothers and fathers will stay with me forever'

'I had no idea things where this bad. None of the media have reported this'

'We are a forgotten war Captain; only important enough for a footnote after the conflict in Syria and Iraq. The West is reluctant to admit it has abandoned us'

Both Englishmen looked at each other. They had both flown Harriers during the Gulf War and had been responsible for their share of destruction and death. It was what they had been trained to do and had put the experience to the back of their minds. Until now.

It was an uncomfortable reminder that dropping a bomb from ten thousand feet had consequences.

'Your fellow countrymen and Miss Deveraux are in the hotel. I will take you there but the two Arab gentlemen are under guard on the top floor of the hotel. It would not do for a member of the Saudi Royal Family to get killed when the government troops advance'

Steele was first to ask the question 'what do you mean'

'My apologies did I not mention there is going to be an attack on the town at approximately o-six hundred today'

Steele looked at his watch; lifting it up to catch the moonlight. The time was o-four hundred.

'My god that's in two hours' time!'

'Exactly Mr. Steele which is why I am taking you to the hotel. It is the only building the enemy will not shell with their British made Challenger Tanks'

The irony was not lost on the two men.

The Captain was first to suggest 'if they know there are European and Arab civilians in the town maybe they will hold off their attack' he suggested.

'Not a bad idea and one I have considered. Let's organise a ceasefire. We can then get all of you to safety. When you are tucked up in bed; the enemy will then be free to obliterate the town and everyone in it. You will be heroes Captain'

Both men suddenly had a very sickly feeling in their stomachs. They were both experienced in the effects of war on civilians who had no way of defending themselves. To walk out of this town knowing it would be blown to hell the minute they left was not going down well.

The jeep pulled up outside the entrance to the hotel.

Khan waited until they had collected their belongings before he spoke 'the young Prince is residing on the top floor. I am expecting a reply from his government shortly. The other Arab gentlemen is also in the hotel but is being kept under guard for the time being'

The two men looked at each other. The Captain shook his head as if to say 'don't say anything'

'I am curious about something though Captain'

'What is that Mister Khan'

'Well' Mohammed said frowning and appearing to look baffled 'I have examined your planes log and the notes you have written. It seems you would only be staying in Spain for a few hours and then departing. It also notes the Arab gentleman would be travelling on with you'

'The travel arrangements of my passengers are no concern of ours Mr. Khan' the Captain shrugged.

'Agreed Captain but I am *curious*'

'Oh, why is that?'

'I am curious about where the most important **Arms Dealer** in the Arab world would be going to; or who he would be visiting'

THE HOTEL

Micky spotted the Captain and Co-Pilot entering the hotel lobby from his balcony and went down to meet them.

The stairs and hallways were only eliminated by the odd burning torch but the full moon helped.

'Hey Captain can you believe this shit'

'I'm glad to see you are well Mister Manning. Is your friend here to'?

'Yes! Manny is trying to get some sleep. Did you know there's going to be a battle soon? Mohammed thinks we will all be dead before the suns up unless we can do something. I just made a video for him. Laid it on thick I can tell you. Bloody government should get their frigging act together before it's too late'

'I thought it was Miss Deveraux who did the video' he asked surprised at the intensity he was showing.

'The French bird did one as well but it was all in her language. Can't see that having much impact on my mates and fans back home can you; so, I did my own. Wait till the *skinny bird* gets a load of that. Could be in line for a knighthood mate and no mistake'

The two men just looked at each other as Micky strolled away looking very pleased with himself.

'Have you any idea what he just said Captain' Steele asked.

'Micky Manning is probably the best player in the Premier League just now. Thankfully you don't need a high IQ to kick a ball around a football field. I'm curious though how Khan persuaded him to help. He doesn't look the bleeding-heart type'

'Did he not mention something about an MBE'

Both men started laughing 'stranger things have happened Jim'

CHAPTER 7
LONDON

The Minister resisted the urge to pace the room. It would not do to show how anxious he was; waiting for the next video to be aired. The phones had been ringing nonstop with Television and Newspapers Editors, Members of Parliament and even one of the Royal Family calling for information. The latter apparently, a supporter of Micky Manning's Football Team. It would get worse after the video was shown.

The BBC news presenter suddenly stopped reading her autocue and announced that a video showing the premier league football player Micky Manning had been received.

THE VIDEO

Is this thing working yet; It is; Hi there all my mates and fans in England; and the other places of course' he began referring to the rest of Great Britain 'the Captain managed to land the plane safely but believe it or not we've ended up in some Arab town that's about to be attacked by their government. They're not like our lot by the way; their Government that is. These guys are real baddies. Mohammed; that's the guy looking after us; told me all they wanted was independence. A bit like the Tartan lot in Scotland. Anyway, they didn't think that was a good idea and decided to start this war. To say it's a bit one-sided is an understatement believe me and these people are starving by the way'

It suddenly dawned on Micky that he was talking about people only a few yards away. Living in shelters and desperate to survive the day.

It wasn't much to ask for surely.

The change in attitude was not lost on the people watching.

I was brought up in the East End and saw a few things I didn't like. The London Riots for example. My Uncle lost his frigging business because of that lot. Killed himself a few months later. I don't know any Muslim's but like most of you watching I considered them all Terrorists or worse. That French stewardess said it all when she described us as ignorant. If Mohammed is right; the attack will begin in just over three hours. If you want Micky Manning to play football for England and win a World Cup; you had better tell the Prime Minister to get off his backside and help'

The Minister was genuinely taken aback at the sincerity the player was showing. Within a few seconds of the finish his secretary's board was lighting up with calls.

'Don't bother putting any calls through there is nothing new I can tell them' he told her.

'But surely the PM is going to do something. The whole country will be up in arms if Manning is killed' she asked.

'Don't forget his Manager and the air crew as well' he said.

'Is there nothing we can do'

'The PM is using every leverage he can but their government is insisting it's all a miss-understanding. They have maintained all along the tribe are no more than terrorists. If they do attack they can claim it was to rescue the *hostages*'

The Minister was aware how an effective PR Machine could turn the tables on them. The intelligence up-date he had just received confirmed that government armour was un-accounted for. In other words, they had no idea where they had disappeared to. The Minister had been in the Army before joining the Ministry. He knew instinctively where they were. Well camouflaged not a mile away from the town; and unless they moved out of their lair it would be impossible to locate them. Until it was too late that is!

'That's it' he suddenly thought going to his secretary 'get me Sir Henry on the phone' he said before moving back to his own desk.

The red button flashed as he sat down 'Sir Henry good of you to call. I was just wondering what the readiness state of our Carrier Fleet in the Med was!'

The MI6 Director advised him.

'Excellent!' he said nodding to himself 'maybe it would be a good idea if the French

Carrier launched a few sorties over the no-fly zone just to show the flag and all that'

The director advised him that was already being considered 'there's nothing like having a young woman pleading for help to get the indignation up. And she just happens to be French and not bad looking. Those sailors aboard The Charles De-Gaul have all seen the video of her. It didn't take too much persuasion for the Fleet Admiral to agree some early *training* sorties!'

The Minister couldn't help chuckling to himself 'dam but that Khan is good' he said again.

THE HOTEL

The guard stood to attention as Mohmmed approached; then opened the door to let him into the room.

The Arab businessman was standing on the balcony looking up at the moon. A cloud obscured its glow for a few seconds then passed by 'I was wondering when you would get to me Mr. Khan' he said not turning around.

'I thought I would leave the most important one until last' he replied.

'But the young man in the suite above is a member of a royal family is he not. I am, after all, just a business man' he answered coming back into the bedroom.

'That is what you want us to believe but we both know different'

The information he had received from America had surprised even Mohammed in its detail. There was no way his friend could have gathered that much background material without the CIA's approval or at least its tacit agreement. The Arab was his Ace in the Hole. If he failed to convince him to help, then the attack on the town would be carried out; despite the indignation of the rest of the world. And that was less than two hours away.

Mohammed looked directly into the face of the Arab and spoke 'in less than two hours the government forces will flatten this town and everyone in it. I therefor do not have the time or the luxury of taking my time interrogating you *Tabarrok Shabbat*'

The Arab tried his best but hearing his real name spoken out loud made him look up sharply.

Mohammed smiled. It was a good start.

'I am aware you have many other names Tabarrok but that *is* your birth name is it not!'

'You seem to be well informed Mr. Khan. That kind of information is known only to a very few associates. Or of course to the western Intelligence Agencies'

Tabarrok studied the man in front of him for the first time 'you have an American accent Mr. Khan; possibly New York?'

'Spot on. My father still lives in Manhattan by the way'

'But I am guessing these are his people; which is why you came to help them fight this stupid war of theirs'

Mohammed refused to be intimidated or get upset at the comment. His CIA training had prepared him for such insults and goading.

The Arab continued his affront 'I have a feeling you have had military training as well Mohammed Khan; if that is *your* real name of course. Let me guess; the American Marines? Not a very prestigious branch of their army. Cannon fodder I think it was called in the first world war'

'You missed out my CIA training Tabarrok. I thought I should mention that just in case you are thinking I can be intimidated or coerced in setting you free. You are the only one from that jet who would have a chance of getting through the government blockade alive. You have after all supplied most of the weapons they are using against us'

Mohammed waited a few seconds before continuing.

What he was about to say would bend the Arab to his will or make himself a laughing stock.

'You would of course wish to take **your son** with you'

The Arab's face suddenly drained of colour 'how did you know' he stammered.

Mohammed had studied all the information he had received very carefully. It puzzled him why such an important figure would chance travelling alone. The most important and wealthiest Arms Dealer in the Arab world would be a target for any paid assassin. At any other time, he would be surrounded by body guards. Dubai was not a Country that spent a vast amount of its wealth on Military hardware. It did however, pride itself on being the playground of the rich. It also offered discretion and security for its many famous guests as Micky Manning could testify.

If Tabarrok was visiting Dubai alone then it could only be for personal reasons. When Mohammed had received the Arab's real name he looked again at the passport photographs. The resemblance was obvious.

The young Prince had to be his son.

Tabarrok sank into a chair completely drained and looked up at Mohammed 'there are only a few people in this world that know Tariq is my son. If my enemies found out; my son would be in great danger. It is also quite possible his mother would be put to death for adultery. You know as well as I do what the law is like in Saudi. It seems you have me at your mercy Mr. Khan. What do you want from me'?

Mohammed felt pity for the man but he would not show it 'where were you going after leaving Spain'

'I think you have already guessed that. I was meeting your Interior Minister to discuss an arms deal. I was to join up with a British Contractor in Malaga'

'The British have agreed to an Arms Embargo. If the UN discovered they were secretly supplying Weapons, it would cause a major diplomatic incident'

'But they're not supplying weapons. They are however; going to supply spare parts for existing weapons. Have you any idea what it takes to keep a battle-ready Challenger Tank in the field. I earn more commission selling spare parts than I do selling the Tanks. You may also be interested to know that without these parts those Tanks out there won't be able to operate'

This was interesting news. It also answered the question of why the General in command was so eager to attack the town. They could have waited another few weeks and the occupants would have to surrender or starve.

Another thought crossed Mohammed's mind. Inside the downed aircraft, he located a small lap-top computer. A model he didn't recognise but something like the ones supplied to CIA Agents in the Field. It was pass-word protected so there was no way to access the information.

'When you realised the plane was going to crash land did you contact anyone?'

'I mustn't underestimate your investigation skills Mr. Khan. The answer to that is yes. I have a very efficient Security Director. I would think he will already be on his way to this country to mount a rescue. He will be most upset to find I am already dead'

'And your son as well!'

'He will of course not be aware of his existence or the fact an attack by the army is imminent I agree'

'You appear to be taking this situation in your stride Tabarrok. If it wasn't for that young man above I would think you were willing or even ready to die'

'Again, you are very astute. I have survived numerous assassination attempts. I think the odds are against my living until old age. But you are correct. The death of my son would weigh heavily on me; so, I will ask you once again. How can I be of assistance'?

Mohammed sat on the bed and looked squarely at the Arab 'I don't care what you promise or have to pay. Call your Contact in the Government and get him to stop this attack'

'I will need access to my computer'

Mohammed went to the bedroom door and opened it. The guard outside passed him the computer.

Tabarrok almost laughed 'I must never underestimate you Mr. Khan' he said again taking the lap-top.

'I think the internet connection is still working but call me if you have any problems' he said leaving the room.

There was nothing else Mohammed could do but wait. The life of his friends and the towns occupants where now in the hands of Allah.

CHAPTER 8
THE ENEMY

General Abdul Hakam Saran blew smoke into the air from his Cuban cigar and felt at peace with the world. Allah had delivered to him the possibility of a great victory over his enemies. In just over half an hour his beloved Tanks would rise from their carefully concealed lairs and rain death on the Town. There had been talk amongst his underlings that it may not take place but he ignored their defeatist talk.

An Aide entered his private tent and saluted smartly 'there is an incoming call from our beloved Minister of the Interior General. He insists it is urgent' he almost shouted it due to his nervousness.

'He probably wants to congratulate me' he replied waving his cigar in the air like the Cuban Dictator Castro; one of his heroes.

Saran went to his desk and switched on the screen. The Minister came to life and he saluted the image.

'General Abdul Hakam Saran it is good to see you. The President himself sends you his greetings. I wouldn't be surprised if he was pinning a medal on your chest in a few days' time. You have achieved great victories over the separatists; but we believe now is not the time to attack the Town itself'

The General's chest visibly deflated. He had miss-heard surely?

'But Minister there will never be a better time than now to eradicate these traitors' he almost shouted.

'Never the less General, the President has agreed with my decision. Stand down your troops and return to base. That is an order'

The line went dead.

It took a few seconds for the General to comprehend what had just happened. He went from indignation to anger in less than a minute. This was wrong. It must be a mistake.

He picked up the monitor and physically hurled across the tent. It smashed against a desk and shattered the screen.

The Aide rushed in to see what the commotion was all about; then left just as quickly.

The General checked his watch. It was o-five twenty-five.

What had happened to make the Director of Interior change his mind. What had he missed.

He went over his battle plan one more time. Nothing had been left to chance...except!

'I should have destroyed their communications centre when I had the chance' he realised 'something must have happened in the town itself. Surely it had nothing to do with that Private Jet crash landing' he thought.

The more he thought about the more it made sense and the angrier he became. He had failed. The talk of medals was a sham.

He would not be allowed the same freedom again he was sure of that. Too many other Generals with better connections would take his place.

So be it. If I am to be replaced, then I will have my victory.

He shouted for the Aide.

'Yes General' he asked saluting again.

'Get me the Commander of Red Section on the secure radio' he ordered pointing to a coloured pin; on a map; spread out on the table.

The Aide had the sense not to ask why and left.

The telephone rang and he picked up the receiver 'Commander this is General Abdul Hakam Saran. I have a special mission for you. You have been chosen to lead the attack on the Town. You will break cover and advance to within five thousand metres of the perimeter. That will put you in range of your target. You are to fire at the Hotel that we have so far avoided. It is their only surviving communications centre. I want it destroyed. Do you understand Commander'

The answer was yes.

'Then may Allah be with you'

THE HOTEL

Mohammed checked his watch again and scolded himself for being so nervous. There was nothing more he could do. It was time to get everyone down into the basement including the stranded passengers and crew. He did not want their death on his hands.

He knocked on a door.

Claudia had been dozing fretfully but that didn't stop the smile appearing on her face when she saw who it was.

Mohammed tried his best not to notice the open blouse and the body behind it. Her hair had fallen around her shoulders. She had no make-up on but her eyes where alight with passion. Even with her arm in plaster and the obvious stress she was under; she was still a very attractive woman. And desirable.

'I need to get you to safety' Mohammed said collecting his thoughts.

'Do we have time Mohammed'

'There is still twenty minutes to go. I think so'

'I did not mean that' she sighed pulling her blouse further apart to reveal her ample breasts.

Mohammed took an intake of breath. There had been no woman in his life since the death of his wife. For once he hesitated, unsure of his emotions.

He was about to reply when the first shell smashed into the building.

Claudia screamed in fear and flung herself at Mohammed for protection.

A few seconds later the door of Micky and Manny flew open.

'What the fuck was that' Micky shouted as he ran into the corridor.

Another second later and Captain Carrington and his Co-Pilot rushed into the corridor as well.

'That was a shell from a Tank if I'm not mistaken and trust me I know the difference'

'The bastards have started the attack early' Micky swore.

Mohammed thrust Claudia into the football player's arms who for once didn't notice the state of the almost naked female.

'Everyone get to the basement. Make sure she goes with you!' he told Micky.

'Leave her to me mate. Where will you be going' he asked.

'There are children in the rooms at the end of this corridor. I must get them downstairs' he said rushing away.

Claudia struggled to free herself but Micky was having none of it. In one motion, he hauled her over his shoulder and ran for the stairs closely followed by the rest.

As they reached the end of the corridor the second shell smashed into the building.

Mohammed had collected over ten small children and was ready to run down the corridor to follow them.

Claudia looked on in horror as the ceiling between them collapsed sending dust and debris towards them.

She screamed in horror and feinted.

Micky didn't stop. He continued down until he reached the basement and then stopped. It was pitch black. The shells had taken out the generator and lighting system.

He was still wandering what to do when a light appeared in the form of torch. More lights appeared as the occupants lit candles or switched on portable lights. It was not the first time these people had taken refuge in a shelter.

Micky handed Claudia over to a group of women. They made her as comfortable as they could and offered them some water to drink.

Micky thanked them and tried to drink the water. It stuck in his throat. It wasn't the dust in his mouth that was the problem; more the shame he felt at dismissing these people as mere images on a television screen.

They were real and he vowed never to take things for granted ever again.

An old woman shone a torch into a corner. A group of children huddled there clearly terrified. One whimpered pitifully and was scolded by a boy not more than five years old.

'Christ' Micky swore as his heart went out to them 'dam it Micky get a fucking grip of yourself and help them' he said to himself.

He moved over to the corner and made the sign he wanted them to part so he could sit down between them.

They complied.

He leaned against the wall to try and get as comfortable as he could. The children looked on suspiciously. This man was a foreigner and they had no happy memories from people like him. They backed away.

'Now ladies and gentlemen the first thing to mention is that I don't speak a word of your fu!!!……' he bit his tongue 'a word of your language' he finished 'which still doesn't give me the right to swear in front of children. My old grandad would have given me the slipper for sure you can bet on that. What we have here is the perfect opportunity for a story. Now as I don't know *any* children's stories I'm going to talk about the only thing that's of interest to me. That's football. Well it also includes women but I guess you're a bit too young to understand all that yet'

He made sure he had their attention 'Now; football is called the beautiful game because that's exactly what it is. Forget about cricket and golf. They don't come close. Scoring a goal will make sixty thousand supporters erupt. There's nothing to compare trust me. And would you believe they pay me a shit load of money. Sorry about that!' he said referring to the swear word.

The next salvo of shells smashed into the building.

Every floor above the basement was now in ruins. The whole building came crashing down on top of them. It also completely blocked the entrance to the basement. The occupants were trapped. More important; there was no fresh air getting in.

Micky ignored the commotion and the pitiful cries of the women as they realised they were all trapped.

There was nothing he could do about it.

He clapped his hands in the darkness to get the children's attention 'now like I said scoring a goal in front of sixty thousand fans is something else; and Micky Manning has scored his fair share believe me' he said continuing his story.

CHAPTER 9
THE MEDITTERANEAN CARRIER FLEET

The two Dassault Mirage F1 Fighter Jets swept across the sea towards the coast of Africa. Within a matter of minutes, they had reached their maximum speed of Mach 2.2. At 6500 feet, they levelled out and reduced power. The fighters carried amongst other weapons; 2 AIM 9 Sidewinders and two GBU-24 Laser Guided Bombs.

The mission briefing had been short and to the point.

'Make sure that young woman down in the town knows we haven't abandoned her' the Carriers Commander had suggested.

It was a mission to do just that. Until the call came over the radio.

'*Scorpion Red seven this is Eagle in the Sky do you copy*' asked the tactical specialist on board the Nimrod Spy Plane flying above.

'*Eagle in the Sky we hear you loud and clear. We are ten minutes out. ETA the town is ten minutes*' he repeated expecting the usual roger and out.

'*Scorpion Red seven we have targets on the ground moving towards the perimeter; do you copy*'

The French Commander suddenly pulled himself up in his seat. That was not what he had been expecting '*I copy Eagle do we have business to attend to*'

'*Roger that Scorpion Red seven we confirm two Tanks have left their lair and have fired on the town. You are cleared to engage. I repeat you are clear to engage'*

The Commander switched over to the Jet flying parallel *'Red six did you copy that'*

'Affirmative Commander. It looks like the Diplomatic efforts have failed. That's a British Challenger's down there and we both know what fire power they have. They will reduce that town to rubble in no time'

'Affirmative. Switch to Tactical and arm weapons. Follow me. We're going in'

'Roger that'

The leading Tank Commander had followed his Generals orders and moved to within five thousand metres of the town. The digital fire control calculated the range to the target. All the Commander had to do was press the fire button. The first salvo blasted out of the rifled barrel and screeched on its way. It couldn't miss. The gunner re-loaded and signalled all was ready. The next salvo hit its target; at least what was left of it.

He was just about to order the next salvo when his tactical console issued a warning of approaching aircraft.

The Challenger two is armed with a L94A1 chain gun and a 7.62 mm machine gun and a chain gun mounted on a pintle. The Challenger can also mount a remote weapon's system bearing a 7.62mm machine gun and a 12.7mm heavy machine gun and a grenade launcher.

The pride of the British Army could look after itself. If it had an experienced and professional crew that is. It hadn't.

The Tank Commander dithered and desperately tried to remember his training. It was too late. The first bomb impacted the turret. The second ripped the tracks apart making the Tank skew sideways. It was a testament to the Challengers special armor plating the crew where not killed outright.

The second Tank suffered the same fate but the damage had been done. The Hotel was in ruins and everyone in the basement was trapped.

CHAPTER 10
LONDON

The MI6 Director had been supplied with an update every five minutes. He was pleased with the destruction of the two Tanks but a little sad the armor was British made. He was aware of the deal being brokered between the Agent and the Government Interior Minister and had raised no objection. This attack on the town had been unexpected. The odds of that deal now going ahead was minimal.

A technician entered his office 'we have an update from the Nimrod; Sir Henry'

The Director switched his screen on again. The Nimrod had over flown the Town. It was in ruins. The cameras had then focused on the burning building that was once the town's only hotel.

'Christ those Tanks have done a number on that building. Was there anyone in it at the time'

'We believe all the people from the plane where housed there. There is no way we can verify if anyone survived'

The Director slammed his fist on the desk 'I've had enough of this. I don't care who we upset we need people on the ground. Get me the Minister on the phone but before you do get that Relief Plane at Braze Norton in the air'

'There is another a lot closer Sir Henry' he reminded him.

There was a French C-17 Globe Master on standby at Base d'Abu Dhabi. He would call his French counterpart; he did and was told the Aircraft had already taken off. It was loaded with supplies. It all also carried a platoon of French Paratroopers to secure the airfield.

The Director thanked him and asked him to call if there was anything he could do to help. He also advised him the Hercules Transporter was on its way as well. It would not carry troops but it would transport two Field Agents to confirm if the Arab Arms Dealer was still alive.

He was, after all, one of their own!

THE TOWN

The Globe Master Transporter made two passes over the town to make sure the inhabitants realized they were not the enemy. It also gave the Pilot a chance to examine the airport's runway. He had landed on worse; so, he gave the thumbs up to the French Major in command of the Paratroopers.

The Transporter rumbled down the runway and came to a stop.

The ramp slowly lowered and the Paratroopers piled out of the plane and spread out. When the Major confirmed his troops were in control of the surrounding area he gave the all clear. The long awaited and desperate supplies had arrived.

One of the Town's Elders approached and welcomed the Major and his troops 'my men will stay well clear of the airport' he informed him.

'I have been asked to confirm the crew and passengers of the Private Jet are safe sir' he told him.

'I am sorry to tell you they; and many others are buried in the Hotel ruins. My people are trying to clear the rubble but there are many heavy boulders and steel girders to move. I'm afraid there is little hope we will find them alive. The air inside the basement must be almost gone'

The Major was just about to inform the Elder that a small bulldozer was amongst the things they had brought with them; when there was a commotion behind him.

'***Let me through***!' a young woman was screaming at the soldiers holding her back.

The Major sighed and signaled to his men to comply 'unfortunately Sir we have brought a news crew with us'

'No apology needed Major' he answered.

The news crew consisted of a female reporter, a cameraman and a sound technician. They had been together for many years. Within a few minutes the female reporter was sticking a microphone in the Majors face and asking about the fate of the French stewardess. It was all she needed to go charging off down the rubble strewn street leading to the Hotel; filming everything in sight.

Within five minutes of reaching the Hotel the satellite dish had been set up. The camera was on its tri-pod and the filming could begin.

FRANCE 24 – We have the news! A Special report by Brigitte Perec; World News Today.

'We have just arrived at the besieged Town in North Africa where the Private Jet crashed not more than twenty-four hours ago. We have been informed by the Town's Elders that the crew and passengers were staying in the Town's only surviving Hotel. The world was led to believe a cease fire was in force and the Government Forces surrounding the Town were being recalled'

The camera panned sideways and zoomed in on the devastated Hotel.

'This is the result of their callous and criminal act. We understand that British made Challenger Tanks opened fire at point blank range (the Minister in London blanched at that comment) destroying the last remaining refuge of the town's women and children. It also housed the crew and passengers of the downed aircraft'

The Reporter continued her report. Within one hour every news station in the world was airing her story.

CHAPTER 11
RESCUE – THE HOTEL BASEMENT

Captain Carrington was seriously worried. It was obvious the air was getting stale. It also appeared no-one was doing anything about it. The communications technicians manning the Control Centre had begun the impossible task of moving the rubble. All that happened was it caused another cave-in injuring three of them.

'If we can't find a way to get some fresh air in here we're as good as dead' he told his Co-Pilot.

'I was just thinking the same Captain. There's no way we're going to dig our way out and you can't expect those poor bastards up there to move all that rubble with their bare hands; that's if they even have the strength to do it. Do you think the Town's been taken'?

'If it has we're as good as dead anyway Jim'

Manny had been listening to their conversation 'we were down here earlier. If I'm not mistaken there should be piping and ducts running the length of the basement. This place doesn't have an underground car park so the ducts should go directly to the outside. I wasn't always a Football Agent by the way. If we can break open one of these ducts it might be enough to get some air from the outside. That's if it hasn't been covered up or blown apart.'

'We have nothing to lose by trying. What we need are tools. There's no way we can undo the mountings with our bare hands. Does anyone speak any Arabic?' he asked hopefully.

'No but this young kid here speaks English. He can translate' Micky Manning called from the corner.

The Captain shone the torch into the corner. What he saw amazed him. The children were clinging to the Football Player as though their life depended on it. The young boy in question had been translating his story. The children loved it.

'Can you ask your mates if they have any tools Abdul' he asked him.

'I will ask' the boy said scampering away and returning a few seconds later 'they have a tool kit. I explained what you wish to do. They will help'

The housing on the ducts were removed one by one. On the third attempt, fresh air suddenly flowed into the basement. Cries of relief and Allah be praised came from the men and women.

For the first time in a long-time Micky Manning uttered under his breath *thank God!*' and meant it.

'All we can do know is wait' the Captain declared.

RESCUE

The bulldozer was small but powerful. Within minutes of arriving on the scene it was dragging away large boulders and iron girders. The soldiers knew time was running out for the people trapped under ground but they also knew one mistake could bury them for good.

The camera crew kept filming. The Reporter kept up the commentary. The next two hours would see the occupants escape certain death or they would be retrieving bodies. **The World** held its breath.

The basement had been plunged into total darkness as one by one the makeshift lighting was extinguished. It made the shaft of light that suddenly came from the entrance even more blinding.

There was a call from outside in French and then in English.

The Captain tried to respond but his throat was dry and it came out in a croak but the rescuers heard it.

The digging continued in earnest. People were alive down there.

Twenty minutes later two experienced Paratroopers climbed inside. They were followed by a Doctor.

FRANCE 24 – We have the news! A Special report by Brigitte Perec; World News Today.

The camera once again panned towards the hotel ruins and zoomed in to the opening made by the rescuers. It was a Reporters dream come true. The first to scramble out of the ruins was none other than the English Football Player. He was covered in dust. He was unshaven. His clothes were ripped and covered in grime. His carefully groomed hair was plastered to his head but he was grinning wildly. More important; so, were the posse of **young children** clinging to him.

The French Reporter was almost lost for words but she recovered her composure and approached the Englishman for an interview.

She asked about the conditions and what was it like trapped underground with no idea what was happening above.

He responded politely and explained all he cared about was that the children would survive.

Manny couldn't quite believe it was the same man from only a few hours ago, he did know one thing though; Micky Manning Premier League Football Player was a real-life **Hero**!

The reporter thanked him and hurried away. The one she wanted to interview had just emerged from the ruins but Claudia Deveraux wanted to know just one thing.

'*Is Mohammed alive*' she asked an Elder nearby completely ignoring the reporter.

'*I am sorry*' was all he said in faltering French.

Claudia sank to her knees and cried unashamedly. The reporter backed off and signaled the camera operator to cut the feed. She may be a hard nose reporter but she was not heartless. The interview would wait.

The Relief Agencies responded.

Within twenty-four hours Cargo planes were landing with supplies.

The Town would survive.

The first aircraft to lift off would return with the British survivors.

Micky Manning stared out of the window at the Town below.

His Manager was getting worried.

The usual jovial carefree footballer and womanizer was now a quiet and solemn man. They had been through a life changing experience it was true; but reserved and penitent wasn't a good image.

He should have known better.

Micky suddenly sat up in his seat.

'Frigging hell Manny wait till the *Skinny Bint* sees me on the television! She's going to be all over me I'm telling you. **Bloody hero** that's what I am'

Micky looked across at his Manager and grinned 'don't worry mate. Your **Micky**

Manning hasn't gone far' he said winking at him.

Manny burst out laughing.

The tears were streaming down his face.

He shook his head and settled back in his seat.

In moments, he was fast asleep. Everything was well with the world it seemed.

THE TOWN

Once the UN accepted there was no immediate threat of hostilities they gave the go-ahead for the Relief Operation to begin in earnest. Cargo planes were arriving by the hour. A temporary hospital was erected close to the airport building; such as it was.

One of the first patients to be treated was Claudia who was perceived as a heroine in France. She was in no condition however to understand the praise being heaped on her; but that would change after her arrival home. Her experiences would be invaluable; in her new career as an actress.

Two men stood on the tarmac and watched as the chartered air ambulance took off and disappeared into the setting sun.

'It will be a long time before my people forget what she did; but I suppose that was down to you **Mohammed**' the Elder commented.

Mohammed shrugged 'it was the right thing to do Elder. We both know it would never have worked out for us. We are from different cultures and backgrounds. No, it is best she believes I was killed in the Hotel'

'A strange attitude given where *you* came from. Speaking of which; when will you be returning to America?'

'Someone said recently I was not to be underestimated. I think that should also apply to you Elder. How did you know I have decided to return to New York?'

'I would have suggested it myself Mohammed but that was before the *American* gentleman arrived. I assume he is one of their CIA Agents'

'Yes, he is. The Agency want my expertise on Arab affairs. I'm a little flattered they think so highly of me. I feel a little guilty at deserting you though'

The Elder laughed 'I don't remember you being a very skillful builder Mohammed and that is what we need here. Your skills are better served elsewhere. We made the mistake of trusting the UN Security Council to protect us. We will not make that mistake again. As an American Agent with access to world affairs you can warn of us of any impending danger can you not'

It was a simple statement but true.

Mohammed nodded in agreement.

'Just one last thing Mohammed' the Elder asked leaning closer 'what happened to your Jeep?'

Mohammed coughed a little before answering 'I would think that by now it is somewhere across the border; but you need not worry. The person who borrowed it promised to send us a replacement. Actually; he promised a whole fleet of new Jeeps!' he grinned.

'The *Arabs* are lucky to be alive. It was either instinct or warning of the attack that made him collect the young man and make his escape down the fire escape as you did. Goodbye Mohammed and may Allah protect you' the Elder said walking away.

Mohammed took one more look at the devastated town before collecting his few belongings and heading back to the airport. He paused before walking towards the American Transporter that would take him away.

Two men were discussing something in English nearby. They had arrived on the British Hercules transport and had immediately gone about making enquiries on the fate of the jets passengers. They had waited like everyone else to discover the fate of the trapped people in the basement. When the rubble was finally cleared, the medics went in. They had tried to follow them but had been prevented by the Paratroopers. Eventually they had gained entrance but not until all the survivors had been accounted for. There was no sign of the person they had come to find. They would continue the search for another few days until finally admitting their quarry had disappeared.

By then Mohammed was being debriefed by his CIA handlers. There was however; no mention of the Arab's escape. That information was being kept to himself. You never know when it was time to call in a ***debt***

CHAPTER 12
REPERCUSSIONS

General Abdul Hakam Saran packed away his favourite cigars carefully in the mahogany box. It had an image of Fidel Castro embossed in the ornate lid. It was his pride and joy. The order had been given to break camp and return to base but he was in no hurry to leave the now deserted compound.

He was a realist.

Actions had consequences but he had no regrets; just pride for doing his duty.

The tent flap opened 'General Abdul Hakam Saran you are to accompany these men to the Capital' the man told him with authority as he was surrounded.

'This must be important if the Minister of the Interior is here in person. Am I to receive a medal after all?' he smirked.

The Minister snarled angrily 'you are to be charged with treason and dereliction of duty *General.* Your stupid actions have cost me dearly'

'Don't you mean it has cost our **Country** dearly' he snarled back.

'*Take him away*' he shouted angrily then added '**Wait.** Take these with you' referring to the cigar box 'a man facing a ***firing squad*** does have one last request after all'

CHAPTER 13
THE HERO'S RETURN

The British Hercules would transport Micky and Manny as far as Madrid where a privately chartered jet waited. It was then on to London.

Manny had been sound asleep since taking off but suddenly came awake and almost jumped out of his seat 'does this thing have a telephone or something' he asked not expecting an answer from Micky who just shrugged.

'Hey mate can you get me a telephone. I need to contact my office in London' he shouted above the noise to a man nearby.

It was provided and a call was made.

'When we get to Madrid don't give any interviews Micky is that understood. Jesus what kind of Manager am I leaving this until the last minute. The same at Heathrow OK! Any interviews are to be sanctioned by me. I *assume* you *are* going to give them'

'Anything you say Manny you're the boss' he yawned.

Madrid Airport was a media scrum. They left behind a lot of disappointed camera crews with unanswered questions.

London Heathrow was even worse but at least a security screen had been put in place by the Police.

Micky just smiled at the array of camera's but made no reply to the questions that came like an avalanche.

The first interviews had been arranged. Sky News first then a visit to the other TV Stations around London.

Manny's office telephone and his private mobile had been buzzing non-stop ever since they had landed. What had amazed him was that his client was already on the front cover of every daily and national newspaper in the country. In fact; all around the world.

Micky Manning Premier League Football Player was now an International Celebrity.

One of the newspapers was on his desk. He picked it up and once again shook his head in wonder at the picture.

The self-proclaimed playboy was emerging from the ruins of a hotel clutching a dozen children. They were clinging to him as though their lives depended on it.

Manny just smiled 'if you look closely my face is somewhere in the background. And long may it stay that way' he said to himself.

Manny O'Brien did not seek or want publicity. A man from Northern Ireland sometimes had a past you did not want people to know about.

He dropped the paper back on the desk suddenly remembering his clients request as they flew back from Madrid. The first game of the season was in five days' time. He needed to make sure the specially embroidered football shirt would be ready for the match.

It just happened to be a local London Derby so a capacity crowd was expected.

THE MATCH

It had been an exhausting week for both men and Manny had to call a halt to the interviews three days earlier. The Manager of the club was sympathetic but he wanted his star player fit for the first match of the season. He had already missed the pre-season warm ups. Manny had ordered his client to rest and stay in bed. He had forgotten the Super Model girlfriend had arrived back from Spain and was on catch-up; sexually that is!

On the day of the match the visiting team had taken the unusual step of calling in to the home teams changing room. Micky was genuinely touched by the sincere congratulations they all gave him.

While both teams were in the same room he made a request. There were no objections.

At the tunnel entrance both teams waited for the go to enter the football ground. The noise outside was deafening. Over sixty thousand fans waited for the hero of the hour. He didn't disappoint them and walked onto the field; ***alone.***

The crowd slowly became aware something was about to happen.

The singing. The chanting. The whistles. It all stopped.

Micky waited until he was sure he had their attention. The stadium that was moments ago, filled with noise, was now silent.

Micky Manning began his speech;
'Only a few days ago, I was trapped in a hotel basement; in a town in Africa. I thought I was going to die. Like many of you in this Stadium I considered people; who were of a Muslim Faith; to be no better than terrorists; or just plain ignorant. They are not. They are people like us. They have families and friends and all they want is to live in peace'
Micky lifted his arms in the air so everyone could see his specially embroidered football shirt.

'On this shirt, I have embroidered the names of twelve children. They were the ones I helped from the rubble of a ruined hotel. In a town, I had never even heard of. They are orphans; but I promise here and now I will do everything in my power to make sure their suffering does not continue. Today I will make that start. Everything I earn from today's match will go to a Relief Fund set up in their honor'

He paused to make sure he had their full attention.
'When I was trapped in that basement I told the children a story. It was all about the beautiful game we call football. It was about the glory of scoring a goal. It

was about playing for your country. But more than anything it was about the cheer from over sixty thousand football fans in a stadium like this'

He paused one last time.

'SO......WHAT ARE YOU ALL WAITING FOR!' he shouted at them.

The football supporters responded by erupting in crescendo of cheering and stamping of feet.

Manny O'Brien was on his feet cheering with the rest. It would be a long time before he forgot a small town in Africa.

BOOK 2

THE RETURN OF KHAN

CHAPTER 1
HOMECOMMING

Michael Khan ignored the monitor that indicated which carousel his flights luggage could be collected. The only thing he carried was a hold-all. It held all his worldly possessions.

His plane had arrived at JFK Airport on time.

The Officer checked his credentials at Passport Control and asked him to wait. Michael made no comment and did as he was asked. A few minutes later his American Passport was handed back to him. Inside was a printed note. He opened it.

Meet me at the new coffee shop just inside the airports entrance.

Michael shrugged. He had been expecting a more formal approach. The CIA after all were aware he was arriving today.

He slung his bag across his shoulders and marched away. The Officer frowned but made no further comment. If it hadn't been for the official request from the CIA; he would have been tempted to check the man out more closely. He did after all look more Arab than American.

He had a point. Khan had not seen a bathroom for many weeks. His hair was down his shoulders. He had a three-month-old beard; and he still wore his Arab robe. He also looked dangerous; even with a friendly smile.

Khan made his way to the coffee shop. There had been a few changes since he left he noted. Not least the security presence. It was discreet but his trained eye spotted at least two armed plain clothes police officers; walking the entrance to the Airport.

It was to be expected he thought given the current threat level.

He glanced around the foyer looking for the new coffee shop. Whoever had written the note must have forgotten it had been a few years since he was last here.

That thought made him realize; he hadn't had a decent cup of coffee since then.

Katherine Carter watched as Khan approached. She hardly recognized her ex-lover such was the change in his appearance. No! not just his appearance she decided. It was everything about him. If she had known about the passport controller's thoughts she would have had some sympathy with them. Mohammed Khan did look dangerous.

Katherine collected her bag from the chair next to her and looked up expecting to see Khan again. He had disappeared.

She walked out of the coffee shop in a panic thinking he had not been given the message. She looked around; desperate now for a sight of him; and not just because it was her job to escort him to a meeting. The minute she saw him the old feelings had returned. After all this time, she was still in love with him.

Katherine pulled out her cell phone intent on making a call but the voice behind her made her stop.

'Hello Katherine Carter' the male voice said.

She spun around annoyed at his trickery; but the annoyance disappeared as she considered his eyes. They had seen and witnessed many things. Not all good.

'How are you Michael' she asked then remembered his change of name 'or shall I call you Mohammed now?'

'Michael is fine. At least while I'm in New York' he told her.

'Very good. Michael, it is. My Director wishes to meet you; but he will understand if you wish to visit your family first' she told him; trying to sound all business despite her pounding heart rate.

'I would like a cup of coffee if that's Ok with you'

'Oh! Of course, let me order you one' she said opening her bag for some change.

'If I remember correctly **your** coffee wasn't that bad?'

It took a few seconds to understand what he was asking.

She took a deep breath before she answered 'actually I've just purchased a new percolator. I think this is a good opportunity to try it out' she shrugged but smiling.

Khan rubbed his chin 'and maybe I can use your bathroom'

THE APARTMENT

Katherine had started making the coffee after showing Michael around the apartment. He had been in the bathroom a good half-hour. She had decided a glass of wine was in order. In fact, two glasses. Anything to calm her down. Her mind and her imagination where on overdrive.

She had just got herself under control when Khan came out of the bathroom.

'Oh Hell!' she could only say as she witnessed the transformation.

Gone was the Arab robe. He was clean shaven. The untidy hair was now tied back in a ponytail.

'I hope you don't mind me borrowing this bath robe' he said sniffing the sleeve 'nice perfume by the way!'

Katherine dropped the glass of wine onto the table; rushed over and kissed him passionately while removing her clothing.

Khan responded by biting her lip in a frenzy of wanting. They reached the bedroom and came together.

HOURS LATER

Katherine rested her head onto Michael's chest. Their love making had been frantic and unrestrained. She had lost count of how many times she had climaxed such was the intensity.

She would have liked to believe it was all her womanly appeal that had done it but during their lovemaking a woman's name was called out by Michael. I don't think he even realized he had said it she demised. She now remembered the woman's name. She also now understood it had been the name of his wife.

Khan felt the mood change in the woman beside him 'if there is anything you want to know; just ask' he whispered.

Katherine rolled onto her back a little annoyed she had been so obvious. But she had to know 'do you still miss your wife'

The question had been expected. At least during his up-coming de-briefing with the CIA phycologist.

'I'm sorry that's not a fair question' she said attempting to sit up.

Khan pulled her back and told his story.

'I first met Ayla at an uncle's house. It was their attempt at match-making' he laughed remembering the meeting 'Ayla was a bit too strong willed for her own good the family decided. She had already rejected two suitors. I was their last hope. They needn't have worried. I fell for her the moment I saw her. Fortunately, she decided I was better than nothing; so, we got married'

'And had a child in very short time if I remember correctly' Katherine butted in.

Khan stayed silent for a few minutes recalling the first site of his child.

'I'm sorry Michael. If it's still too painful I will understand' she said hugging him.

'No! It is time I moved on Katherine. The anger and the pain can eat a man from the inside if he is not careful. Strangely enough I did not blame the soldiers that carried out the bombing. They were misguided and only following orders'

'I do not think I would be so forgiving' she told him.

Khan shrugged 'it was the will of Allah'

The reference to Michael's religion made her uneasy. She knew of course he was Muslim but in the past, they had never mentioned or discussed it. It shouldn't have mattered now but she still felt guilty at thinking all Muslims were potentially dangerous people or even terrorists.

'Are you sure you don't want to visit your father first' she asked.

'No! Let us get the de-briefing over with first' he decided.

CHAPTER 2

CENTRAL PARK; THREE DAYS LATER.

Hassan Khan rubbed his chin thoughtfully. Something his son Michael also did when considering something important.

His opponent opposite didn't rush him. Chess was a serious game and needed thought. He also realized that Hassan was not concentrating on the game.

Word had come through his son was home and visiting today.

Hassan finally made his move.

The Judge; as he was known as; tut tutted and moved his Queen; check mate I think'

Hassan shook his head at such a stupid move.

The Judge stood up. It was an unspoken rule the winner moved to another opponent of his choice.

'Maybe this young man would like to play you' he asked him smiling.

Hassan shrugged.

'Hello father!' Michael said sitting down opposite.

Hassan held his breath for a moment as he pulled out a hanky. He would not cry. It was not the; *done thing;*

'How are you son?' he only asked.

'Pleased to be back. I'm glad you're in good health father'

'And why shouldn't I be. I'm not the one dodging bullets and cannon fire' he scolded, instantly regretting the outburst.

Michael nodded in understanding. His father had been distraught at the idea of losing his only son. He had openly wept at hearing of his daughter-in-law's and his grandchild's death.

Like most Americans and people around the world; he had watched the news as the events in North Africa unfolded. The name; Mohammed Khan had been mentioned more than once by the television newscasters and in the papers. After the cease fire; speculation had mounted the man who was responsible for saving the town was dead. It was only after two days and a call from a young woman he learned his son was still alive.

'I thought you had died Michael' his father told him.

'I'm sorry I couldn't get word to you sooner. It was necessary for certain people to believe I was dead. All that matters are I saved the town from being wiped out'

'We all watched the woman and that football player make their appeals. Was all that down to you'

'They helped but in the end, it wasn't them who stopped the tanks'

'One day you must tell me the whole story. What are your plans now? I expect it is too much to hope you would take over the business I expect'

'We have been through that many times before father. I probably know all there is about jewels but it is not the profession for me we both know that'

'In that case I will sell the shops and just trade the market. An investor has already made an offer'

'Then take it, and retire properly this time. Take up golf or something'

'I get out of breath walking around the park. I don't think so. But you haven't answered my question son!'

Michael paused before answering. His father was not going to like his reply.

'I'm back with the Agency'

'So, that's why you delayed your visit to see me. I thought you had done with all that business'

'I had, but if it hadn't been for the information they supplied the town would have been lost'

'So, you think you're indebted to them?'

'Not indebted, but it made me understand I can't save the world on my own so to speak. I should have known that from my days with the Marine Corps'

'You will make your own way in life Michael I know that but please take care'

He was tempted to suggest it would be nice to have grandchildren again but decided that memory was to raw.

Hassan stood up.

Michael stood up.

'I trust you are not proud to give your father a hug' he smiled 'and there are a few of our friends just waiting to say hello'

It was the cue for all the other chess players. One by one they approached to give their best wishes and condolences.

Michael thanked them. It was good to be home.

KATHERINE'S APPARTMENT

Michael sat up and leaned his back against the bed-head. It was a wonder it was still intact he thought smiling; given the pounding it had received over the past three weeks.

Katherine had risen early.

Michael had sensed the change in mood but had made no comment. Whatever was on her mind she would tell him eventually.

The eventually had come last night.

'Have you any idea what this meeting is all about tomorrow?' he had asked casually.

She was a highly-trained operative that had been taught to conceal her feelings but this was personal. It was also going to be hard to say.

'You know I have been given strict instructions not to tell you, but in truth I'm not sure myself what's going on'

Michael believed her 'OK!' he said studying her reflection in the bedroom mirror 'now tell me what's bothering **you**?'

It was unfair question. He already suspected what the problem was.

Katherine sniffled and grabbed a tissue close by.

'Stop playing games Michael it's not fair on either of us' she retorted a little annoyed.

The past two weeks had been a taste of heaven; emotionally; but it was about to come to an end. In truth, she could continue the relationship; but that meant only one thing. She could not be his *handler!*

'If my Director finds out how deep my involvement is; I would never be allowed to be your CIA contact we both know that. I couldn't abide not knowing what was happening to you in the field!'

Michael had nodded in understanding.

This would be their last time together. They had made the most of it.

Katherine was tempted to kiss him goodbye but she restrained herself.

'I will see you in the meeting later' was all she said; disappearing out of the door.

CIA HEADQUARTER: LANGLEY VIRGINIA

Khan had been impressed with the building and its function on his first visit a few years ago; at least what he had been allowed to observe that is.

He now recited the CIA's unofficial motto.

And you shall know the truth and the truth shall make you free!

He almost laughed. The truth; or at least a version of it had saved the town in North Africa.

He entered the building and produced his ID.

The guard instructed him to wait.

A few minutes later a young woman arrived and escorted him to a conference room.

Katherine met him at the door and showed him to a chair 'the rest of the party will be here shortly. Would you like anything to drink Michael!' she asked politely.

'Thank you, Miss Carter, I'm fine' he answered soberly: more for the benefit of the recording than anything.

A few minutes later two men entered the conference room. One was a well-dressed and distinguished looking man in his late fifties.

He introduced himself.

'It is good to see you Mister Khan. My name's John Cohen; Director of Operations. I will call you Michael if that's OK? I feel I already know you from all that's been happening lately. Hell-of-a-job you did in North Africa by the way' he beamed shaking hands.

The second man coughed clearly annoyed at the delay.

The Director just scowled 'this is *Mister Smith*'

Mister Smith was not the friendly type it seemed. He just nodded in his direction and took his seat.

John Cohen began the meeting. He opened a blue file in front of him.

'First; on behalf of the CIA let me welcome you back in the fold so to speak. The headshrinkers have passed you fit for duty. They were quite impressed with how you coped with all the stress of being cut off in that town, and under siege for so long by the way'

Khan made comment.

'What do you know about Myanmar' he asked him casually.

Khan wasn't expecting a geography test but he happened to know quite a lot about the country.

'Myanmar; officially the Republic of the Union of Myanmar was once known as Burma. It is bordered by Bangladesh, India, China, Laos and Thailand. Its Capital City is called Naypyidaw and its largest City is Yangon, formally Rangoon. Is that sufficient or shall I go on'

Katherine suppressed a smile.

'Err! No that's fine' the Director replied a little caught out 'what I should have asked is; what do you know about the political state of the country'

He was just about to reply but the Director stopped him.

'Forget I said that. Bloody stupid question. You probably know more about that region than any of us'

He looked across at *Mister Smith* expecting comment or input. None came so he carried on.

'I will not give you a history lesson on Iraq or Syria either' he stated 'let's just say the end is hopefully in sight for the so called Islamic State. That does however pose a question. Where will they slink off to when they realize the game is up'

Khan wasn't sure if the Director was asking a question or just making a statement so he didn't respond.

'Recent events lead is to believe a terrorist cell is setting up camp there. This cannot be allowed to happen. What we need is someone who can speak the language. Someone who can mix with the local populace. What we need is up-to-date intelligence'

'What you need is a *Muslim*' Khan butted in.

'Good; Yes, that would help of course' the Director agreed not realizing Khan was being sarcastic.

Mister Smith still made no comment.

Khan studied him more closely.

'I appreciate what you are saying Director but surely you must have well-trained operatives that can do the job just as well as I can. I would even suggest it's a job for one of your own Special Ops Team. Maybe you could even station a spy satellite over them. I don't see what one man can do that they cannot!'

'We've already done some of that Michael. Kathy will fill you in later if that's ok. There has also been attempt at inserting an agent into the area but that has come to nothing' he said once more glancing at Mister Smith.

Khan immediately picked up on the wording. The Director had deliberately avoided using the word **we** in that last part.

Something was now beginning to make sense.

He was also beginning to realize he was not being told the truth why he was here. It was time to ruffle some feathers.

What happened to the operatives' he asked bluntly?

The Director was now noticeably irritated by the lack of input from *Mister Smith*.

'There was in fact only one agent involved. The other people were civilians. The female agent posed as a partner to the Professor. There was a bit of difference in their ages but they came up with a **reasonable** enough cover story 'he said; emphasizing the **word** and again omitting the **we** part.

'What was he Professor of?' Khan asked now completely sure he wasn't being told the whole story.

'He was a Professor of Archeology and a qualified Surveyor'

'And who exactly were these **other** people'

For the first time since the meeting began *Mister Smith* looked at the Director.

'There was only one other person that is missing. She is a Doctor working for the Red Cross' he stated as matter of fact as he could.

Khan stood up.

He leaned across to Katherine and said 'I thought that all the rivalry between the Department of Defense and the CIA was finished with. When *Mister Smith* wishes to inform me why I'm really here; I will return'

With that he left room; leaving a stunned conference room behind.

In the corridor, a young man in a smart suit jumped to his feet; then relaxed when he realized it wasn't his boss.

Khan gave him his best smile 'looks like the meeting could go on for a while; sorry about that'

The young man shrugged 'so what's new' he laughed then became concerned he had over-stepped the mark.

Khan laughed 'I hope they've got you sorted out with some refreshment. Do you want me to get you anything'?

'That's kind of you but I'm OK' he said indicating a hold-all next to his seat.

'I guess working for the Department of Defense is not easy especially with a boss like yours'

'Oh, Director Wyden isn't so bad. Being his Aide does have its perks'

Khan wished him well and wondered away to find the Men's Room. He only had to wait five minutes before Katherine came to find him.

'They want you to return' she told him.

'I guessed they would. I suppose now I'm going to find out why you've been so tight lipped' he said as they walked down the corridor.

Halfway down he commented; '***Kathy***'

'Sorry what did you say' she asked innocently.

'He called you ***Kathy***'

Katherine stopped dead in her tracks 'we only had dinner a few times. He only wanted someone to talk to'

'**Talk to**! Is that right!' he said walking away smiling 'is his *wife* deaf and dumb then'

Katherine followed him back into the room fuming with herself for confessing her relationship with a married man.

Khan re-took his seat and waited.

This time *Mister Smith* did the talking. There had obviously been some heated discussion between the two men.

'You have been an Agent with the CIA long enough to know that some things must remain secret Mister Khan. This is on a need to know basis' he stated importantly.

Khan stood up again. This was so much bullshit.

'First Mister Smith; or should we know start calling you; **Assistant Director Wyden** from the Defense Department; I am under **Contract** to the CIA; which means I can accept or decline any mission I see fit. As you think I'm not qualified to be a need-to-know I decline this mission. Whatever the **hell** it was!'

Khan stood angry with himself for losing control. He was about to head for the door when *Mister Smith* stood up.

'The Doctor kidnapped is my **Step-Daughter** Khan' he shouted.

Michael stopped in his tracks. That was unexpected.

Wyden; as he would now be called slumped back into his chair. The man seemed to age in front of their eyes.

'You need to tell me everything Director Wyden or this will never work' Khan stated.

Wyden nodded and began his account of what had happened.

'Her name is Miranda Robson; my wife was previously married but she divorced after only one year. My step-daughter; has always been a bit of a tom-boy. Very head strong so to speak, but smart with it. Her grandfather has supported her in whatever she chose to do in life. They have great admiration for each other.'

'Is that **Senator** Wyden?'

'My father, yes. Mandy qualified here in New York and immediately registered with the Red Cross to do relief work around the world. She wanted to go into research so it made a little sense at the time. We were horrified when she wanted to help in Africa with the Ebola outbreak. Fortunately, they rejected her offer on the grounds she wasn't experienced enough. A year later she called us from Myanmar telling us not to worry and she was doing fine; helping the refugees in the North of the country.'

Khan interrupted 'was your step-daughter aware of the political instability of the country. Trade sanctions have been in place since nineteen eighty-nine due to human rights abuse. They have only recently been lifted'

'The Red Cross say they made her aware of it but that wouldn't have stopped her. The problem was; she ended up in the Rakhine State'

That was bad news.

'Rakhine has seen long-running tensions between Buddhists and the mostly Muslim Rohingya minority. The recent attacks on some military outposts has led the government to close the border with Bangladesh. When the fighting starts, they will have nowhere to go' Khan stated.

'What the Director said about a terrorist cell by the way is true' Wyden continued 'what concerns me is the abduction of the agent. If this is a kidnapping, there may be a chance of paying a ransom. If I do; my career is over of course' he admitted.

It said something of the man's character that he was willing to sacrifice his career for the safe return of his step-daughter Khan thought; but something was wrong!

He sat back in his chair and rubbed his chin deep in thought.

Katherine watched him do it and smiled inwardly.

'I understand what you meant about the agent being discovered. If they find out she is working for the Department they will kill her. If they then connect her with the others they are as good as dead as well. How did they all end up in the same place anyway?'

Wyden coughed now clearly showing his nerves 'it was on my orders the agent visited the hospital where Miranda was stationed. I asked her to make sure she was OK. In the end, it had the opposite effect. It was my fault she's been kidnapped'

'But why send a Surveyor'

'To check out the *diamond mine*' he replied.

'***What diamond mine?***' Khan almost shouted clearly annoyed at the lack of information.

Director Cohen butted in 'There have been rumors for some time that diamonds have been discovered in the area. We haven't seen any on the market yet but our geologists tell me it could be years before it produces anything worthwhile. There have also been rumors of a large Jade find as well'

'It isn't rumor any longer! Sorry Director but I was going to fill you in later' Wyden said 'the last report from the Surveyor said a block of Jade has been unearthed in a nearby state. It is rumored to weigh over one hundred and seventy-five tonnes. I have no idea what that relates to in terms of dollars!'

Khan made a quick calculation 'One hundred and seventy million in dollar terms' he quoted; greatly impressing the three-people present.

'Jesus if that's what the Jade is worth; what would a bucket full of diamonds sell for' the Director surmised.

'It would definitely finance a terror cell that's for sure' Wyden agreed.

Khan still wasn't convinced. This did not fit the profile of a terrorist organization. For one thing, the Myanmar Government had a very strong military presence that could block any IRAQ type incursion. The country was also dense forest in most places. Not easy for moving large numbers of men. No something was off!

He suddenly sat up in his seat 'where was this professor's university' he asked Wyden.

'It's in California. Why do you ask?'

'Can you get someone down there to make enquiries?'

Wyden looked at the Director 'I still have my contacts, unless you can arrange it?' he asked him.

Khan frowned and looked questioningly at Katherine.

Wyden explained the comment 'I had a call from my office before this meeting. My Director is asking questions about why one of his senior analysts is on extended leave. This operation had not been cleared by him you understand. I cannot tell him just yet. He will pull me off the search if he knows I am personally involved!'

'He will have a point Director if you don't mind me saying' Khan said.

'Agreed but it means there is no chance of any further investigation. Officially they are not there at our request'

'That could work to our advantage'

'Why do you want to make enquiries into the Professor by the way. Are we missing something?'

'I also want the same enquiries made at your step-daughter's hospital'

'Miranda! But why. Surely you can't believe she's involved in some way' he asked getting angry.

'Nothing of the kind I assure you' he answered calming the man down 'I want to find out if enquiries have been made as to their authenticity'

It was Katherine who caught his drift 'if there has it means they want to confirm their identities. That could be a worrying development Michael' she told him.

'What Katherine is trying to say is this. A terrorist cell wouldn't be bothered in finding out who the people they kidnapped were. We all know the profile of a terrorist group and what their aims are. This doesn't fit the bill. These people especially the Surveyor were taken for a reason.'

'They want him to survey the land where the diamond mine is located' the Director jumped in 'My god! We have been so focused on this being a terror plot we have ignored the obvious.'

'It does mean also, Miranda is still alive. I would be very surprised if you *do* receive any kind of ransom demand.'

It was some comfort at least.

Khan continued 'If I'm correct in my assessment it begs the question who is behind all this? The first thing is to confirm enquiries have been made. If by e-mail; we could possibly trace the senders IP address. I think that one is wishful thinking. If by telephone; again, we may be able to trace the call if we can narrow down the call time. 'The worse scenario is a *personal* visit'

'Why?' asked Wyden not understanding his logic.

'It means these people have agents operating inside the US. It means they have the funds to finance it. If this wasn't the work of a terrorist organization, it could soon turn into one!'

The CIA Director turned to Katherine 'you have my authority to use whatever assets you think fit; but low profile. Do we understand each other?' he asked her.

She nodded.

He turned to Khan 'Shall I arrange transportation to Myanmar?'

'No Director, I will make my own way there via Cairo!'

'**Cairo!** I don't understand' he asked, then put his hand up to stop the reply 'Don't tell me just do it. Katherine is your contact of course; but I am available if you need me. Is there anything else you need now?'

'Not right now Director, but maybe we could have an extraction team on standby!'

'Let me work on it. Come on Wyden we need to talk' he finished standing up to leave.

Khan waited until the room was clear.

'Sorry about that jibe earlier it was uncalled for' he told Katherine.

'It's all in the past Michael. A silly mistake. You were brilliant by the way' she said smiling 'and are you now going to explain about Cairo?'

'I wasn't convinced all this is about terrorism; but I was serious when I said it could turn that way. Not the fanatical ISIS Ideology type of thing; but a much more sophisticated organization. If I just drop into the area and start asking questions I wouldn't last five minutes. What I need is an ***invitation***!'

CHAPTER 3
CAIRO; EGYPT

Aapo Farouk took a long drag from the Hookah Pipe and sighed deeply. Everything was well with the world he decided; as he watched his third wife flutter her eye lashes on the couch opposite.

'A man does what he has to do I suppose' he sighed; relishing in the thought of the night to come.

The little bells on the bamboo partition tinkled as they were pushed aside. A manservant entered.

'You have a visitor master' he announced solemnly.

'Not now you fool. Send him away I'm busy'

'But Master. You have told us many times that if this man should call he was to be admitted immediately'

Farouk immediately threw the Hookah to one side '**Khan is here**?'

'Yes Master'

'Then show him in you babbling idiot' he said dusting down his robes to meet his visitor.

'I trust this is not an inconvenient time to call Aapo Farouk' he said looking at the beauty on the couch.

Farouk shooed the woman out of the room unceremoniously. She pouted and wiggled her ample bosom making the jewels on her bodice sparkly in the candle light.

'It is good to see you again Mohammed Khan; if you are still going by that name that is?'

'For this meeting, I am; but when I leave it will be another name. May we speak in English. It will take me a while to re-learn the nuances of your dialect'

'Of course, my friend. Come in and sit down. I will order tea' he said clapping his hands to attract a servant.

The two men sat opposite each other. Khan waited for the obvious questions.

It didn't take long.

'I searched the whole of Cairo to thank you. I will do that now; he said solemnly bowing to the man opposite.

'How are your two sons?' he asked touched by the man's gratitude.

'They are alive and well. We both know we have you to thank for that'

THREE YEARS EARLIER

A BAZAAR IN CAIRO

Khan had been in Cairo for over six months but he had yet to find the men he was searching for. The CIA had placed them on the top twenty most wanted list. He was in danger of failing in his mission and being ordered to return home.

He was frustrated but still believed he was making headway. The two young men opposite bore testament to that.

Abdel and his younger brother Akbar Farouk were the sons of a wealthy and influential merchant; who also happened to have the best spy network in the country; and beyond. The meeting was to discuss plans of a trip to America. The recent relaxing of the Marijuana Laws in California could mean big business for the Farouk family.

The meeting had been planned for early in the morning to avoid the summer heat. The three men sat around a table waiting for drinks to be served. The coffee shop would normally be very busy this early in the day; but the owner had cordoned off the entrance to any customers. He would be well paid for his lack of business.

The brother's minders where still drowsy from the night before. It was probably the reason they did not spot the armed men racing across the square until it was too late.

The four guards were gunned down before they realized what was happening.

Khan however; was as alert as usual.

He instantly assessed the situation noting the lay-out of the coffee shop.

The gunmen would need to enter the coffee shop through the front doors. They were wide and now fully open but there was still only enough room for them to enter two at a time.

He waited.

The gunmen had focused all their attention on the two brothers who had jumped to their feet to witness the commotion outside.

It was a fatal mistake.

Khan stayed crouched as the two men entered. Victory and a big pay-day was in sight. They still ignored the man in front of the brothers; who was seemingly cowering in fear.

Without warning a gun appeared in his hand.

Khan was a trained killer. The men were amateurs.

The first assailant staggered backwards as two bullets ripped his chest apart. The second attacker still couldn't comprehend what was happening until it was too late. A bullet shattered his collar bone.   Khan instantly adjusted his aim. The man collapsed in a heap as another bullet tore into him.

Khan again assessed the situation. Another gunman had come in behind the first two and was levelling his Kalashnikov. The two brothers were still frozen to the spot unable to move. They were sitting ducks.

He leapt over the coffee table and rugby tackled the two men sending them both flying backwards into an alcove behind them. The wooden lattice screen shattered as they fell through it. If the third gunman had been a professional, he would have realized all he needed to do was move to his right and he would have a clear shot. As it was the alcove obscured his view. In frustration and anger her fired his weapon at the wall.

Chunks of plaster and lattice work flew everywhere.

Khan waited.

The gunman emptied his magazine and discarded it.

He was fast; but not fast enough.

Khan stood erect and levelled his weapon. He just smiled as one bullet made a hole in the man's forehead. He put one in his chest just to make certain.

The men outside had seen enough. They rushed back across the bazaar and disappeared into the many narrow alleyways.

It was over.

Khan lifted the older brother to his feet and dusted him down. All he could do was stare at the carnage around him. That was until his younger brother groaned in pain.

Akbar's robe was turning red there was blood oozing from a wound in his shoulder. Khan swore in Arabic and bent down to examine him.

He looked up 'we need to get out of here before the police arrive. Do you have a safe-house nearby?'

'Yes' he answered attempting to help his injured brother.

Khan waived him away 'I will carry him. Just lead the way'

The safe-house was only five minutes away but it seemed to take forever. The way fortunately was clear of people. They seemed to have just disappeared when the shooting started.

Abdel ran up to a heavy wooden door and banged the large brass knocker.

A pair of eyes appeared in a slot in the door.

Abdul ordered him to open the door, they entered and Khan dropped the brother on a bed. He was also now covered in blood from carrying him over his shoulder. The man had moaned and howled in pain but it couldn't be avoided.

Khan reached into his boot and extracted a slim but very sharp knife. He cut away the robe around the shoulder to expose the wound. He was expecting a bullet hole. Unfortunately, it was much worse.

A wooden splinter protruded from his shoulder. Khan touched it causing another howl of pain from the young man.

'We have to get this splinter out or he will bleed to death'

'I have sent the man for a doctor' the older brother sobbed.

'Your brother will be dead before he gets here' he said making his way to the kitchen.

Khan lit the gas ring on the metal stove and placed the dagger in the flames. What he needed to do would cause great pain. He needed a gag; otherwise the man would probably bite his tongue off. He tore through the cupboards and drawers.

Nothing.

He was running out of ideas when he noticed the wooden chair nearby. He walked up to it and karate kicked the back of the chair. It shattered. Khan then smashed the remaining back rest on the stone floor. He had his gag.

You need to sit on your brothers' chest to stop him moving. What I am about to do will cause him great pain. He will fight us.

Khan tested the knife. It wasn't hot but it would have to do. He dug into the wound. The young brother squirmed and bucked as the knife opened the wound. He continued to probe until he was sure he had loosened the splinter. When he was satisfied he carefully removed the splinter and tossed it into a bowl nearby.

'The doctor will want to examine it' he told Abdul who was in danger of collapsing himself.

Instead he ran to the sink and vomited.

Khan went back to the stove and once again heated the blade. This time however until it was glowing red. He returned to the bedroom and without warning placed the blade on the open wound. The searing of flesh once again made the brother dash to the sink.

The younger brother was now unconscious. He would remain that way for another five days.

'I am ashamed of my weakness' Abdul croaked when he returned.

'Don't be. I have seen bigger and stronger men than you faint at such sights. You did well Abdul. I trust your brother will recover, but he is in the arms of Allah, is he not' he smiled moving to the door.

'**You are leaving**?' he asked astonished 'but my father will want to reward you. What you did in that coffee shop was incredible'

'My reward is your safe return to your family. Goodbye Abdul'

The Father would stay by his sons' bedside for the next five days. The wailing of the woman around the bed was ignored. On the fifth day, his son opened his eyes. The father wept openly and kissed his sons' hand saying a prayer as he did so.

He went outside completely exhausted '**my son will live**' he announced to the gathered family.

The wailing turned to tears of joy.

The Father raised his hand to quieten them.

'The man who saved my children has chosen to disappear. So be it; but heed this. If ever Mohammed Khan returns to us he will have anything he desires. This I swear!'

Farouk would never forget his promise. The man who saved his children was now in front of him.

'What do wish from me Mohammed Khan. If it is in my power I will do it' he vowed.

Khan produced a passport and passed it to him 'my name from now on is Mohammed Suleiman. I am a collector of antiques and dealer in jewels especially diamonds. I want the whole of Cairo to know my name and why I am here especially anyone connected with the diamond trade'

'This I can do, anything else?'

'I want a line of credit at a Cairo Bank'

'How much?'
'Ten Million Dollars'
'It will be done'

The man didn't even blink at the amount.

'I will return your passport to you tomorrow. It will contain the account details of the bank. Where are, you staying?'

He told him.

'Thank you Aapo Farouk' he said, extending his hand.

The man took and kissed the hand 'do not be a stranger to us Mohammed'

CHAPTER 4
THE HOTEL IN CAIRO

It was considered the best hotel in Cairo.

It ought to be; the money it's costing per night Michael thought as he discussed business with yet another merchant.

It had been like this for the past four days. Farouk had certainly got the word out he was open for business. But he was beginning to wonder if his plan would work.

A man in a white suit entered the hotel lobby. He approached the desk and asked a question. The clerk pointed in his direction.

He ignored his approach.

The man coughed politely 'Mister Mohammed Suleiman?' he asked in a crisp cultured accent.

Michael pretended surprise 'Yes sir, that is me.'

'My apologies for such a rude introduction and the fact I have not called to make an appointment. My name is Hassan Hamid and I deal in rare artifacts and precious jewels. I would wish to discuss business with you.'

Michael sighed 'it has been a long day Mister Hamid. Let us make a time for tomorrow. I am just about to eat my evening meal' he said pointing to the restaurant.

'Maybe I could join you Mister Suleiman? It would be on me of course.'

'We have only just met Mister Hamid. I do not make a habit of dining with strangers.'

The mans' calm demeanour was wavering at the idea of being rebuffed. He was not used to such treatment.

He clicked his fingers and a large muscle bound man approached.

'Maybe this will change your mind' he said handing over a small diamond.

Michael feigned surprise again but accepted the jewel. Like a magician, he suddenly produced an eye glass. He polished it with a small handkerchief and placed it is his eye.

He took his time.

'I do not understand where this came from' he said frowning 'and believe me I have visited almost every diamond mine in the world'

The man smiled and relaxed. If he had pretended to guess its origin he would have recovered the gem and walked away.

'That is because the mine is undiscovered Mister Suleiman. Now do I have your attention?'

Michael nodded 'you are paying?' he said just to remind his dinner guest of his offer.

The meal was excellent. The conversation kept in general terms.

His guest drank water.

Michael drank wine 'A vice I acquired in America I'm sorry to say Mister Hamid. I apologize for my weakness' he said hiccupping.

'No need Mister Suleiman, I assure you. What is New York like. I have never been to America' he asked.

'I wonder to behold that's all I can say. Take my apartment for example. Four three two Park Avenue is the second tallest sky scraper in New York. The view my friend is incredible!' he beamed importantly.

'You are indeed a lucky man sir' he agreed.

Michael stared at his guest 'let us get down to business, shall we? What do you want for that gem of yours and how do I purchase more of the same?'

'You are the expert sir. What price would you place on one so rare?'

Michael pretended to calculate the price 'I do have clients willing to buy such a gem.' he conceded 'I will add on my small finder's fee of course.' he shrugged; hiccupping again 'I would think one hundred thousand US Dollars would be a fair price.'

Hamid nodded. It was exactly the price he had already been quoted. If he had any doubts about this mans' expertise they had been dispelled.

'A fair price Mister Suleiman but I am afraid the gem is not for sale just now. It is the only example I have. I'm sure you understand'

'Of course, never mind. I will ease my disappointment by purchasing a nice Jade Artifact'

Suleiman looked across the table at his dinner guest. Maybe he could still do business after all but possibly without his other clients knowing about it.'

'You have a liking for **Jade;** Mister Suleiman?' he asked as casually as possible.

'Not a liking Mister Hamid. **A passion**!' he sighed 'It was my first purchase as a dealer. My father did not think it was worth the money I paid. He was right of course, but I just had to have it. Another weakness of mine I'm afraid!'

'I see' Hamid said smiling in understanding 'maybe I could be of help in this area. I happen to know a large piece of Jade has just been uncovered. Would you be interested in knowing more?'

'Come, come Mister Hamid don't tease me. There have been no decent Jade finds in years. What I wouldn't give to see one' he sighed, hiccupping again.

Hamid had taken the bait.

'If there was such a find; would you be interested in seeing it?'

Michael replaced the wine glass on the table. The bottle was now empty. He stared at the man opposite.

'You're serious! There is such a find' he said slurring slightly.

'Indeed, there is Mister Suleiman'

'When can I see it?' he demanded.

The man shrugged believing he was now fully in control of the meeting 'It **is** possible but forgive me for being blunt. Do you have the funds to purchase such a gem?'

Michael dug into his breast pocket and opened his wallet. He tried to pull out one business card but only managed to scatter the whole amount over the table. He just ignored them and began writing on the back of one.

'These are details of my Bank in Cairo and New York; Mister Hamid. I think my credit will more than satisfy you.'

Hamid nodded his thanks.

The meeting was over.

Michael waited until the man and his Minders had left the hotel before pulling out his cell phone.

He was completely sober. A large tip to the wine waiter earlier in the week had ensured he was never given a bottle of wine that contained anything but flavored water.

The call was answered on the first ring.

'He took the bait Katherine'

'Not before time. I've just seen the bill for that hotel you're staying in.'

'The CIA can afford it. How did the enquiries go?'

'You were correct in thinking they would check out their hostages. It is what you feared. A person approached the University pretending to be a relative. The Professors name was already on the notice board so I don't think they delved too far. The same goes for the Doctor'

'Have you made sure our man in New York knows what to do?'

'Don't worry we have used him before, he knows what to do.'

NEW YORK

THE NEXT DAY; 432 PARK AVENUE.

The concierge stamped his feet and clapped his hands. It was only Autumn but the cold weather was already here. He looked up at the sky and got a face full of rain for his troubles.

He took off his cap and knocked the droplets away. Nothing was going to interfere with his smart appearance. It was his job to look the part. His customers; the people living in the skyscraper behind him expected nothing less.

He didn't notice the man behind him until he spoke. It was not usual for the occupants to arrive other than by taxi or limousine.

'Winter is coming early I think' the man said from under his umbrella.

He spun around and doffed his hat 'my apologies Sir; I didn't see you leave the building. Do you wish a taxi?'

'Yes! I need to go down town. I came to visit a friend but it seems he has gone away. Do you know Mister Suleiman?'

'Without a doubt, Sir. A fine gentleman he is for sure. Are you a relative?' he asked noting the slight ethnic appearance.

'No just a friend' he answered none committal.

The taxi pulled up to the curb.

The concierge didn't give the visitor a chance to object. He snatched the umbrella.

'Let me take that sir while you get out of this rain' he said opening the taxi door.

The visitor handed over a ten-dollar bill and got in.

The concierge waited until the taxi had disappeared before looking up at a CCTV Camera discreetly located nearby.

He put his thumb up.

That little piece of theatre had just earned him a large bonus from the Government Agency that paid him.

CHAPTER 5

CIA LANGLEY

Katherine thanked her FBI counterpart for attending the meeting. The concierge had done a good job and had been well paid. They not only had a picture of the person's face but also his fingerprints. It had not dawned on the man getting into the taxi he had not retrieved his umbrella; until he was well on his way. It would have looked very suspicious ordering the driver to return; and anyway, it wasn't important he thought.

The CIA were not tasked with following up on domestic investigations hence the reason for the visit from the FBI. The Agent had been given the bare facts behind the request.

She had suggested he was a man of **_interest._**

Katherine had worked with the Agent in the past. He had accepted the story at face value with the understanding he be kept updated on any further developments.

She thanked him and escorted him to an elevator, as it was on her way to see the Director.

The moment she entered his office she knew there was a problem.

The four-star General stood up as she entered and introduced himself.

Ten minutes later she walked back down the same corridor but in a very different mood.

It seemed their new President had begun blocking any CIA Operations not sanctioned by the White House. The Director had thanked the General for calling to see them in person.

When he had left the office, she rounded on him 'what am I to tell Khan?'

'Tell him the truth Katherine. Khan will understand. If he wishes to abort the mission that's up to him. Remember; he is under Contract.'

'We both know he won't do that if the hostages are still missing.'

'How did they find out he was over there?'

'They didn't and still don't. It was our request for military assistance that got the Defense Department suspicious. They put two and two together and started making waves; politically that is. The problem is Katherine, we still cannot confirm they **have** been kidnapped!'

'But they have been missing for over two weeks now.'

'That's the point I'm making. **Missing** not officially kidnapped. There has been no ransom demand has there?'

'If Khan decides to continue with the search will we still support him in the field?' she asked getting angry.

'Of course, we will. The CIA does not abandon our operatives just because the political scene has changed. Mind you, a less expensive hotel would help!' he grinned.

Katherine apologized for getting angry.

The Director sometimes had to walk a political tightrope but his priority was always the men and women out in the field.

'Has Khan arrived in Myanmar yet?' he asked her.

'Yes Sir. He checked into the hotel last night. He was told to expect a package with instructions on how to reach the Jade mine. The man in Cairo was a little annoyed he couldn't organize his transport but had insisted on a certain hotel as they are footing the bill.'

'A little good news at least. Just one thing before you go' he said stopping her leaving 'we may not be able to put a team on the ground but that doesn't mean we can't use other assets at our disposal in an emergency.'

Katherine wasn't quite sure how a Nuclear Attack Submarine could be of help; but she kept it in mind.

MANDALAY; MYANMAR

HOTEL ROYAL CITY

The hotel boasted three stars. Not quite up to New York standards but he had seen worse.

Khan had arrived at Mandalay International Airport by Private Jet late in the evening. He had kept his arrival secret to allow time to arrange his onward journey.

The agent in Cairo had offered to provide transport but he had insisted on being independent.

The offices and warehouses of Tiger Imports were located not far from the terminal.

Khan entered the reception and rang a bell on the counter. A young man appeared from behind a desk and bid him welcome.

'The owner is busy in the office, please take a seat while I call him' the young man suggested.

He complied and sat down as indicated.

He wanted the camera on the wall opposite to get a good picture.

He refrained from winking. This was not the time for frivolity.

The owner duly appeared a few minutes later 'Mister Suleiman! Welcome to Myanmar. Please follow me' he said leading him into the office; then into another room with no windows.

He closed the door behind him.

Sorry about all the cloak and dagger stuff but you can't be too careful around here. Even the dam shithouses are bugged by the military around here. Let me get you a drink'

'I'm fine Mister Cogan'

'Call me Johnny. It's good to hear a New York accent occasionally'

'Despite the fact, I look like an Arab Merchant' he asked smiling.

'Well there is that. You do look the part by the way.'

'I have lived quite a few years in North Africa. I have family there' he said by way of explanation 'Have the Agency been in contact?'

'This room is secure' he advised 'Langley contacted my two days ago, with your list. I was intrigued with one of the items you wanted.'

'If all goes well I won't need it but it's a backup plan. Well; sort off' he laughed.

'I was told to expect someone out of the ordinary' he laughed as well 'I guess they were right.'

'Does your helicopter have the range to reach the Northern Province' he asked getting down to business.

'The NH 90 has a range of eight hundred km. If you are talking about reaching the border I would need to re-fuel.'

'I will call my contact and make sure that's available. Have you flown in that area before?'

'Only once and nearly got shot down for my troubles. A Q-five Fantan Jet made its presence known by firing off its twenty-three millimeter cannons. I didn't need a second demonstration'

'There's much unrest in that area; so, I suppose it would be feasible to have air support. Is there a military base up there?'

'There are about five or six around the country. I'm not sure which one is the closest to the border. Is it important?'

'Not for now. I'm expecting instructions from the Agent tomorrow. I will let you know the co-ordinates of the Jade mine when I have them.'

'I hope this man of yours has clout with the military. I don't fancy another run-in with those MIGs.'

Khan went through his plan and what he expected of the agent. He was confident Cogan would do his part, but also suspected the man wouldn't risk his life for nothing. After the meeting, he had been shown around the warehouse nearby. It seemed Tiger Imports was doing quite well for itself.

'We supply most of the hotels with wines and spirits. You can't imagine what a good bottle of bourbon sells for here. Same with most other luxury goods.'

'You seem to be doing well Johnny. I see you employ a few local women as well' he said nodding in their direction.

Cogan just laughed 'it's a perk I never get tired of. Hey; are you interested in a little **fun** while you're here?'

'Another time maybe' he replied.

'No problem, just call me anytime' he said 'it's my way of getting over my *divorce*.' he finished looking sad.

'I'm sorry to hear that. Was it recent?'

'It was over **ten years ago,'** he laughed hysterically.

THE NEXT MORNING

Michael collected the package from the clerk at reception the next morning. He would have breakfast and consider his next move.

There was a commotion in the bar adjacent to the restaurant. He ignored it until he heard an American accent. A man was demanding a drink at the bar. **Very loudly**. He dismissed it as another example of his countryman's bad manners. The retort from a female asking him to keep quiet however made him investigate.

He entered the bar and stopped dead in his tracks.

Milling inside was the **Professor** from California; and the **Doctor** from New York.

'What the hell?' he asked himself.

'Professor please calm down. Your blood pressure must be through the roof. The young man at reception will return our passports as soon as he has checked us in' scolded Doctor Robson.

For people who have been held captive they look in remarkably good health Michael thought; but where was the **female agent**.

She entered; moving around him. He was almost blocking the entrance.

'Do you work here?' she asked in **Arabic.**

Getting no response, she asked **'Do you work here?'** in **Burmese**.

She was about to ask in another language so he stopped her 'maybe we should talk in English Miss Win. Or can I call you Sunita?'

The look of shock at her hearing a New York accent was hysterical but Michael controlled himself.

'Who the hell are you and how do you know my name?' she demanded angrily.

'My name is Mohammed Suleiman, Miss Win. This is not the place to talk. Tell me your room number and I will visit you in one hour' he said looking at the room keys in her hand.

'I don't invite strangers; especially **men** to my room **Mister** Suleiman. Now who are you?' she again demanded.

'Let us say we have the same employer. Have you contacted them yet by the way?'

Sunita took a step backwards and studied the man who claimed to know her. She had no choice but to trust him. Any attempt at calling America would be stupid.

Especially if she asked to be put through to the Department of Defense in Washington.

'No I haven't' she admitted 'these telephones are more than likely monitored'

'Leave that to me.'

The Doctor approached 'are those our keys Sunita' she asked.

Sunita nodded and handed one over.

'You can give that Professor of yours his. My job here is done. Bloody man is a menace. **Who's this**?' she asked looking at Michael.

'Just a hotel employee making sure we have everything we need' she replied getting a raised eyebrow from Michael.

He played the part and just bowed respectfully.

'Pity. Dam sight better looking than that Professor of **yours**' she said striding away.

Sunita was blushing at the comment. She had played her part well but the Professors attentions and **advancements** had been unwelcome and annoying.

'I will see you in your room later. You look as though you need a shower and a good night's sleep'

Sunita looked across at the bar unsure what to do.

'Leave the Professor to me. I assume you *are* in separate rooms!'

Sunita just growled and walked away.

Michael watched her go. He had seen her file in New York but the photo didn't do her justice. Her parents had emigrated from Sri Lanka when she was young. They were both Doctors and quickly established themselves in America; eventually settling in New York. Sunita excelled at college and had considered following in her parent's footsteps but her passion for archeology and languages caught the attention of a Defense Department recruiter.

She was smart and very attractive. More than one suitor had proposed marriage but Sunita was hooked on the life of an Agent. It gave her freedom and a sense of purpose. She loved her job; despite the recent feeling of being abandoned she would continue in her chosen career.

Sunita glanced back as she entered the lift. Michael was still staring at her as the doors closed.

The Professor had now received his drink. A large glass of whisky.

Michael shed his Arab persona and joined him.

'Hey barman' he asked loudly in his best New York accent 'can I get a strong coffee around here'

The Professor took the bait and turned around 'bloody nice to hear a friendly voice at last' he drawled.

Michael feigned surprise 'that sounds like a good old Texas accent if I'm not mistaken. Hi friend: my name is Michael from New York. Let me buy a fellow American a drink. What will you have?'

'Don't mind if I do Michael' he answered downing the whiskey in one 'my name is Professor Howard John Henry O'Hanlon by the way' he announced importantly extending a hand.

'A Professor! This is an honor. What brings you to this part of the world?'

The Professor was just about to answer but didn't. He looked around the room furtively.

'Been on a bit of a little trip for the government if you know what I mean Michael' he said tapping his nose 'can't say too much at this stage you understand but I was paid very handsomely; and not by **them** either.' he grinned.

Michael frowned at that news. His instincts told him the hostages would be found safe and well but this was a surprise even to him.

He wished the Professor well and left; but not before ordering a bottle of champagne and two glasses to his room. A large tip to the waiter made sure the order was kept discreet.

His room, like all on this floor was bugged. He opened his lap top and began compiling a message. The computer had an encrypted programmer which meant that anyone attempting to intercept the e mail would never be able to decipher it.

Back in **NEW YORK**; Katherine Carter couldn't believe what she was reading!

One hour later Michael knocked on Sunita's door. She opened it and let him inside. He put a finger to his lips.

'Hello Miss Win. I wanted to celebrate my good fortune at being in this wonderful country and wondered if you would care to share a bottle of champagne with me' he said walking around the room.

Sunita shook her head and pointed at a framed picture nearby indicating; *that* is where the microphone was.

'Why thankyou Mister Suleiman. It *has* been a long day but a *quick* drink is most welcome' she answered emphasizing the word quick 'my cup of chocolate can wait I suppose'

She had ordered the drink on the house phone.

'I understand you are interested in archeology and rare artifacts' he continued 'that just happens to be the business *I* am in. Maybe you would like a job as my *assistant*' he asked not expecting an answer.

'*I accept*!'

'*What!*' he answered almost spilling the drinks he had just poured.

'I *accept* your offer Mister Suleiman'

'Well that is a surprise' he answered completely taken aback.

He thought she may be play acting, but the look on her face told a different story.

'Let us sit on the terrace and celebrate your appointment then Miss Win' he glowered.

He closed the patio door behind them.

'What was that all about may I ask'

'Who are you Suleiman and who do you work for. Please do not attempt to deceive me. Better men have tried trust me'

Her file did not do her justice he decided again. She was stunning; especially with that look she was giving him.

'My name is Michael Khan and I work for the CIA. My mission/contract was to rescue you from whoever kidnapped you. I was also tasked to discover if there was such a thing as an undiscovered diamond mine; and was it being used to finance terrorism. It seems the first part of my mission is now over. How did you all end up here?'

Sunita accepted the explanation.

She had already concluded he was in the same business as she was.

'Armed men raided the hospital while we were visiting Doctor Robson. At the time, it seemed like a perfect excuse to visit. My Director had asked me to check up on her. I assume you are aware who she is?'

He nodded.

'The Professor forgot to mention he had high blood pressure and a heart problem' she continued 'he needed to replace some tablets he'd lost on the way. The next thing I knew we were being bundled into the back of a truck. The Doctor by the way has balls, she told us both not to try and escape or do anything stupid. If it wasn't for that idiot I would have tried. We reached a camp three hours later. I still had my watch by the way but they had confiscated cell phones and lap-tops. They bundled us into a large tent and told us to make ourselves comfortable. To be honest it was all a bit strange. We were being treated like guests. I would have expected harsh treatment and threats but nothing!'

'I did conclude this was not your everyday kidnapping or terrorist abduction; but that did come as a surprise'

'The next day a man came and invited us to a meeting; in a large tent, nearby. There were guards everywhere but we didn't feel threatened in any way. He then made the Professor and the Doctor an offer. I was considered a hanger on and not worth anything. Fine by me, I thought'

'What kind of offer' he asked pouring champagne into the glass.

'They wanted the Professor to survey the land around the site. It seems the surveyor hired to do the work had become ill. Time was of the essence they said. When I later asked him what they wanted he told me a runway needed constructing and a new road installed to service it. Pretty basic stuff he said'

'You said they made him an offer'

'Yes, they did. Why do you think he's celebrating at the bar? He has a pocket full of **diamonds** in his pocket!'

Michael frowned. This just wasn't making sense.

'Could you find this site again' he asked.

'Sorry no. I was kept in the camp. Navigation and map reading is not my strong point either. The Professor could though' she decided.

He already considered that a possibility but not in his current condition he thought.

'What about the Doctor'

'Doctor Robson was taken away. We became very concerned for her well-being but two days later she arrived back and told us not to worry. She was in a very strange mood. Not her usual happy self. She returned only once to collect supplies. She looked exhausted'

'Did she explain why?'

'Yesterday was the first time I've seen her since then. I did ask what happened but she just shrugged. I had the feeling she didn't want to make things worse for whoever she had been treating'

'Your kidnappers have played a smart phycological game that's for sure' Michael admitted 'by returning you safe and sound it will seem all is well and delay any investigations; not that the military **would**. Someone high-up is definitely protecting these people: whoever **they** are.'

'They are South African or **thereabouts** I'm sure of it' Sunita said 'I couldn't quite place the accents'

'Well done'

Sunita yawned.

'I should let you get some sleep. We will discuss your job application tomorrow!'

'I am serious about coming with you. If you **are** going to finish your mission. What did you mean by being on a Contract by-the-way?'

'A long story. Another time maybe'

Sunita yawned again and stretched her arms out wide. The robe she was wearing fell apart before she had chance to stop it.

Michael stopped himself from making any comment; but hell, that was all woman!

'I will see you in the morning. Goodnight Sunita' he said leaving quickly.

Sunita tossed and turned all night. The last three weeks had been a strain on her nerves. She slept fitfully and dreamed.

A man was chasing her on a beach. The spray soaked her silk gown as she ran. She was laughing because he couldn't catch her. The sand became soft. She had to slow her pace. Suddenly a hand on her shoulder made her spin around in fear. The hand slowly made its way down her neck. To her breasts. To her stomach. To her legs. She now understood. It was not fear she felt. It was **anticipation!**

Sunita groaned and arched her back then waited for the spasm to subside.

Her hand fell away from between her legs.

In an instant, she was fast asleep.

Michael was having trouble sleeping but for a different reason. Sunita was in his thoughts; but now was not the time to pursue that dream.

It wasn't until well after midnight it came to him.

Angry with himself he dressed and rummaged through his travel case. Entry to the room was via a slot card. It registered on a computer in reception when used to open the door. He broke open a sealed plastic wallet. Inside was a similar card; but this one would not register on the computer.

He wedged a shoe in the door to stop it closing and looked out.

A CCTV Camera was mounted in a corner. The corridor went at right angles. A sign on the wall saying LIFT. The camera automatically panned right and left. Each cycle taking no more than six seconds. He was fortunate in that his room was closest to the camera.

He waited and judged the point it was turning away.

Carrying a chair, he placed himself under the camera. Standing on the chair he stood up making sure he was out of the vision of the lens. One hard pull and the live feed would be disconnected. For some reason, he stopped. Something was wrong. The small red light under the camera should be glowing to indicate the camera was on.

'Dam it' he swore to himself.

The chair was tossed back into the room.

He walked quickly down the corridor. Inserted the key in the door and ran into the room.

Sunita was fast asleep but all her survival instincts came alive.

Michael bent over her intending to wake her.

A hand shot out from under the sheets and tried to grab his throat. He grabbed her hand to stop her. Another hand tried to do the same. It was like wrestling with a snake as he attempted to calm her. This woman was a lot stronger than she looked. And well trained in survival techniques.

'Sunita it is **Mohammed**' he whispered as loudly as he dared.

She kept on fighting still drowsy and confused.

Michael would ask himself later why he did it. He kissed her.

Sunita stopped fighting. Her arms slowly encircled his neck. She responded; darting her tongue into his mouth. He groaned in desire but tried desperately not to respond. He loosened his grip and ran his hands down her arms.

The next second he was being tossed unceremoniously off the bed and onto the floor.

'You had better have a ***dam good explanation*** Mohammed or you're in big trouble'

He burst out laughing 'get dressed Sunita we need to check on your Professor; and the Doctor' he said as quietly as he could.

She was out of bed and dressed in seconds.

Michael used the same card key.

They entered the bedroom. He let Sunita wake the Doctor. He didn't want a repeat of earlier.

Doctor Robson came awake in an instant **'Sunita!'**

'Please get dressed and come into the bathroom' she whispered.

They closed the door and flushed the basin.

The Doctor looked at Sunita and then at Mohammed.

'A **definite** improvement on the Professor Sunita' she said smiling at the two of them.

Mohammed couldn't resist returning the smile 'it's not what it looks like Doctor. At least not yet!' he replied getting a quizzical look from the half-dressed woman.

'How are you feeling' Mohammed asked.

'I thought I was the doctor around here. Why do you ask?'

'Have you been in contact with the Red Cross' he asked ignoring the question.

'Of course, they were delighted to know we are all safe'

Mohammed frowned. Maybe he had got this all wrong.

'He did call me back later by the way. Well not my contact it was his secretary'

'Why?' was all he asked.

'He asked me to attend a seminar being held locally. If I was up to it of course. I was intending to travel back to the US but I suppose it can wait a few days'

'Is this the first time you've heard about a Seminar'

'Yes of course. I wouldn't miss an opportunity to hear the ideas of leading researchers on tropical medicine'

'The Seminar is bogus doctor' he told her 'we need to get you out of here and on a plane, as soon as possible'

'Don't be silly. How do you know its bogus? It was the Red Cross who suggested it'

'Did the man give his name and contact number'

'No but I assumed it was the same number I called him on'

'I guarantee if you call the Red Cross they will deny any knowledge of it'

She was about to do just that but Mohammed stopped her.

'If you do. You are as good as **dead**'

She looked at Mohammed. Then at Sunita.

'Who the **hell** are you people' she asked already suspecting the answer.

'My name is Michael Khan but please call me Suleiman while we are in the hotel. I work for the CIA. Miss Win here represents the Department of Defense'

'Did my **step-father** send you to check up on me' she asked angrily.

He didn't let her answer 'she followed her **orders** Doctor just like I'm doing. Your parents have been in turmoil not knowing if you were dead or alive. I think it's about time you dropped this **self-pity** and **anger** regarding your step-father and what he does for a living. Let me repeat myself. If I don't get you out of here by this time tomorrow, you are as good as **dead'** he repeated angrily.

Sunita butted in 'we need to check on the Professor'

The Doctor agreed; annoyed at herself for getting upset. She hadn't yet contacted her parents. This man had touched a nerve.

'The professor is across the hall' Sunita informed them.

Mohammed entered not bothering to call out. As soon as he opened the door he knew the Professor was dead. He was too late.

The room was a mess. Discarded clothing and empty wine bottles were on the floor. The Professor laid naked spread eagled on the bed.

The Doctor was about to check the man and administer aide but Mohammed stopped her.

'No-one has to know we have been in this room. Our Professor had company tonight' he said pointing to a pair of panties under the bed.

'He had high blood pressure and a heart condition. That kind of exercise was the last thing he needed' the Doctor commented.

'There will be a post-mortem; but my guess is; it will not reveal the puncture mark on his neck' Mohammed said pointing to it.

They left the room as they found it.

Returning to his room he opened a case and pulled out a cell phone.

The call was answered on the second ring 'Mister Cogan this is Mohammed. I need you to book flights on the first flight out of here'

'Any particular destination'

'Any safe country with an on-going flight to the USA'

'How many passengers?'

'Two. Doctor Robson and Sunita Win'

'Now wait a minute' Sunita jumped in.

He continued with the details and signed off.

'Don't even think of arguing Sunita. If her step-father found out you let her travel without protection; he would understandably be upset to say the **least'**

She couldn't argue with that and he was her boss.

'Pack just essentials. No suitcases. We don't want any problems when you check-in. With any luck, you should be well on your way before these people realize you are missing'

The Doctor nodded in understanding now 'I owe you an apology Mister Suleiman'

'Not necessary I assure you'

'Visit me when you return to America. I have a feeling there is more to you than meets the eye' she said before closing the door behind her.

Sunita looked at the man she had known only a few hours. The doctor was correct. There **was** much more to this man.

She kissed him 'that goes for me also' she said leaving quickly.

CHAPTER 6
THE JADE MINE

Mohammed stood next to the NH 90 Helicopter on the Heli Pad and watched the Jet disappear into the distance. The Doctor and Win were safely out of the country.

He opened the letter in his hand and read the contents one more time;

Dear Mohammed

Thank you for helping us. I feel a little stupid at being so naive. Sunita asked me more than once where I had been going and for what purpose. I believed that by keeping quiet I would be protecting the innocents. I was taken to a village not far away. (I have drawn a rough map on the back of this letter). It soon became obvious the villagers were virtual prisoners. There was a new compound not far away but I was never allowed to go near it. There had been an outbreak of Cholera in the surrounding area. The villagers were becoming ill daily. It meant they couldn't work in the mines nearby or be laborers for a new road being built. The men guarding them were angry but realized they had to stem the contagion. I did what I could but was hampered by lack of anti-biotics. I tried to explain to the guards I needed the drugs; tetracycline; trimethoprim-sulfamethoxazole and erythromycin. They had no idea what I was asking for. The next day a young woman I took to be a nurse came to my tent and asked what I needed. I was shocked by her appearance. She had cancer but I couldn't say which type. My best guess was radiation poisoning. It was obvious she had been warned not to discuss the compound but I did ask if she had a doctor. Her reply was simply; **dead!**

I managed to control the disease but one of my questions was never answered. Where were all the young girls of the village. The answer came a few days later. A young woman only just out of puberty was pregnant. She had been very ill and needed a doctor. I think the guards were not happy her coming to see me.

I will let you make your own assumptions what was happening.

Goodbye Mohammed.

Mohammed opened his cell phone and called Langley.

Katherine answered immediately.

'Michael; what's going on. We've been monitoring the newscasts and police bands. All hell is breaking loose. The police are searching for two missing Americans. They have also advised our Embassy of the death of the Professor'

'He was murdered Katherine but don't hold your breath on there being an investigation. Even if the Embassy insist on full disclosure it will look like he had a heart attack while humping a local prostitute. The man was well inebriated when I left him at the bar and flashing his money everywhere. I should have seen it coming but didn't until too late'

'What's happened to the Doctor and the Agent?'

'I'm sending you their flight details in a moment. I'm including a letter the Doctor wrote. Keep it to yourself for the time being'

'Why?'

'Because I want to check her suspicions out; before we go stamping our feet and demanding action or whatever we do nowadays'

'I don't like the sound of this Michael. Maybe you should call it a day and come home. You have completed most of your mission and this death is going to cause problems. Not least for Director Wyden. It was he who sent him over there remember'

'The Professor was an accident waiting to happen. In fairness to Wyden he couldn't have known what was going on in that part of the country. Read the letter Katherine' he said cutting her off.

He didn't mention the diamonds. He had been tempted to return to the Professors room but the chance of discovery was too high. The odds of finding the diamonds were zero anyway he decided.

Cogan approached his passenger 'all ready when you are partner. I sure hope your man has cleared our flight path'

'He has trust me. The man wants his commission and this trip is costing him; you can bet on it. Do we have everything I asked for?'

'We sure do. But what you need one of **those** for I don't know' he said pointing to a large canvass container secured to the underside of the helicopter.

'Will it affect your stability'

'No. I've hauled bigger and heavier things trust me'

To the pilots' relief their flight plan had been approved by the Military.

As they approached the GPS co-ordinates Mohammed tapped his friend on the shoulder 'we need to alter course' he said pointing to an x marked on a map.

'That's not a good idea Mohammed. The control tower we are approaching has warned us not to deviate from our flight path. I'm not sure but I think our communications are being blocked. I can't reach my base in Mandalay!'

'In that case, we can blame it on them. Ignore them until we drop of the package. We can then suggest our Gyros and Navigation are being interfered with'

The pilot shrugged and complied.

He reached the drop site and surveyed the surroundings. The X was a small hill strewn by large boulders.

Mohammed put the thumbs up indicating it was ok to release the bundle. He did. With the extra weight gone the machine immediately rose upwards. He adjusted the pitch and looked down. The package was almost invisible amongst the rocks. Now he understood why Mohammed had specified a certain type of camouflaging.

The controller in the tower was getting suspicious but accepted the explanation for the deviation in its flight; for now, that is!

'Look at the control tower' Cogan said as the came in from the North as directed 'the radar is standard but *that* dish isn't. That's a jamming device. No wonder I can't raise my office'

Mohammed took pictures on his micro camera as they came in to land.

Mohammed was met by a man claiming to represent the Agent in Cairo.

'Welcome Mister Suleiman. My name is Joseph Oconto. I have the pleasure of escorting you to the Jade mine'

The man was African but the accent was English.

'You are a long way from home *Major* Oconto' he replied noting the pips on the uniform.

'I have the honor of representing my country in this area Mister Suleiman' he answered, taken off-guard at the man knowing his rank 'we should leave at once. The mine is not far; but the road leading to it has much to be desired'

Mohammed collected his bag and explained it contained the equipment needed to survey the Jade find.

The transport was a Suzuki Jeep; the kind with a roll-bar. He jumped into the back seat and made himself comfortable. The road leading from the compound was newly built. It joined a main road after about five miles. A Security Barrier manned by armed Guards prevented any unwelcome or uninvited visitors. The barrier raised as they approached. The guards waved them through.

'This is a most interesting country Mister Suleiman. Do you not agree?' the Major commented.

'Is it not like your own country Major?'

'It has similarities but we cannot boast the likes of that' he said pointing to a ruined Buddhist Monastery in the distance.

The Major was not going to be drawn it seemed. Mohammed was now sure the man had been educated in England; possibly even Sandhurst their Military College.

After thirty minutes the Jeep slowed down, then turned off the road onto a track. It was blocked once again by a road block manned by armed guards.

This time the barrier stayed down.

An Officer approached and walked all way around the Jeep. He made a show of checking their papers. The brown envelope enclosed in the documents slid into his breast pocket.

He saluted theatrically and waived the barrier open.

The track had seen recent repairs but the Major still had to avoid numerous pot holes.

Mohammed constantly checked his GPS.

He almost missed the track he was looking for.

He now concentrated on the track ahead. They should be approaching a river. It was not yet the rainy season so he didn't expect much in the way of running water. It must however have a bridge to cross it.

There it was.

They slowed down and rumbled across the wooden boards.

He tapped the Major on the shoulder 'I wish to stop a moment. My bladder is not what it used to be' he shouted.

The Jeep pulled up. Mohammed grabbed a small case and trotted off into the undergrowth.

The Major decided to take the opportunity to have a smoke. He leaned against the bonnet and lit his cheroot.

He finished the cigar and frowned. His passenger was taking his time he thought; deciding to investigate.

Mohammed appeared and apologized for the delay.

They set off again.

The block of Jade had been discovered by local miners. Mohammed was genuinely awestruck at the size and quality.

'What my father wouldn't give to be here' he thought to himself.

He went through the process of cataloging the Jade. He would have expected at least the odd miner working the find; but there was no-one around. As casually as he could; he wondered away to survey the area. The Major had stayed by the Jeep. The huts were all empty of belongings. It was clear no-one had occupied them for quite a while.

He had seen enough.

He returned to the Jeep and thanked the Major for bringing him.

They began the return journey.

Mohammed once again checked his GPS. At the wooded bridge, they once again slowed. Half way across he detonated the C4.

The Major was completely taken by surprise as the front of the vehicle bucked upwards. His head crashed against the steering column helped by Mohammed thrusting his hand behind the mans' neck. He was dazed but still conscious. That was until a needle pricked his neck.

The Major slumped sideways.

Mohammed exited the Jeep which was now in danger of tipping over the side and into the river. He pushed the man aside and started the engine. He slowly reversed the Jeep off the bridge and surveyed his handiwork.

The C4 had blown a hole in the right side but there was still room to pass on the left.

His time as a Marine and then being educated by CIA Instructors had paid off he decided.

The first thing to do was make it look like an ambush of some kind.

He propped the Major up in the driving seat making sure his head was tilted to one side.

The last thing he needed was someone querying the puncture wound on his neck. Taking aim, he put a bullet through the windscreen. The bullet made a starred hole.

It also grazed the Majors' neck. He made sure he wasn't bleeding to badly. He fired two more bullets through the windscreen with his hand gun. Making sure one of them impacted the Short-Wave Radio screwed to the console.

Questions would be asked why he hadn't radioed for assistance.

Mohammed drove the Jeep across the bridge and down the track until he came to the turn off he had noted earlier. It was obvious there had been no traffic for quite a while. The undergrowth was slowly eating its way into the track. He drove as fast as he dared avoiding the many potholes. As the track wound its way up the hill; the vegetation thinned; giving him a better view ahead. The mine had been abandoned a few years earlier but the mining company obviously had decided it was too expensive to remove the cranes and other equipment scattered around.

Mohammed checked the Major was still sound asleep on the back seat. Grabbing his bag, he made his way up a steep track. More than once he almost lost his footing on the gravel path but he made it to the top without incident.

Brushing aside the vegetation he surveyed the valley below. This was not the time for sightseeing however. He set up a tri-pod and fixed his camera. He needed as many shots of the valley as he could. Examination and assessment would come later. Satisfied he had everything he moved along the escarpment. He continued taking photographs until he came to a stream which turned into a waterfall; it cascaded down into the dam below.

Packing up he made his way back down the steep track to the Jeep. Dismantling the zoom lens, tri-pod and case; he replaced the parts inside the bag. The casual observer would not recognize the parts as a camera.

He retraced his journey down the old track and was relieved to join the other larger track unobserved.

Now the play acting could really begin.

Skidding to a halt in front of the manned barrier he jumped out and shouted for help. The guards neither spoke Arabic or English but his meaning was clear. The bullet holes in the windscreen did the rest.

Panic ensued.

The Major was removed and placed into a covered truck parked nearby.

Mohammed was unceremoniously bundled into the back of the Jeep. A driver and one armed soldier took over. They set off in a screech of brakes. Half an hour later they reached the compound to find it in a state of panic.

Cogan joined him as he jumped out 'all hell broke loose when they got the call you had been *attacked*' he grinned.

'Let's hope the Major doesn't remember how he actually got the cut on his neck. Let's get out of here. Do we have permission to take off'?

'No, but we can wind the bird up and then call the tower. I'll explain my passenger is scared to death and wants to get out of here'

Permission was granted. They wanted to see the back of their unwelcome visitor.

Mohammed waited until they were well under way before he asked his questions.

'Did you manage to place the box on the tower'

'They had a woman technician look after me ever since you left. When the call came through you had been attacked she rushed off to find out what was happening. The tower is only constructed of metal girders so it was easy to scale the side and locate the power grid on the outside. I don't suppose you're going to explain why I had to do all that are you? Especially as we aren't going to blow the tower up!'

'It's the same reason we dropped the package earlier Cogan. **_Insurance_**'

'Mine is not to reason why' he shrugged.

'Let's hope I never have to use them' he replied not wanting to elaborate further.

'We should be out of the jamming signal in a few minutes. I need to call the office to make sure my unwelcome visitor hasn't decided to pay me another visit'

'Why unwelcome?' Mohammed asked more to make conversation than anything else.

'Every month I get a visit from the local tax Inspector. All routine stuff. I show him the books. He takes his bribe and everyone's happy. Two months ago, a new guy turns up.

Nasty little shit I can tell you. Refuses my offer of a *donation* straight off. Looked the place over good and proper. The next month he came again. Same thing. By this time, I was getting worried my secret office would be discovered. I also wondered why I was under investigation. I made enquiries. Six months ago, a business man from the Capital turned up and purchased containers of high end goods. Whisky; vodka included. He was an Importer like me so why take the hit on buying my stock I thought. The answer was simple. It was less expensive to buy from me than transport the goods all the way from the Capital. It seems he had a Contract to fill urgently as well. From what I have seen today I know now where the Contract came from'

'He was supplying the compound and the other sites around the area!' Mohammed concluded.

'You have it in one partner. I've managed to keep a low profile so far but the competition is getting worse. I think my enquiries got someone suspicions. I also have a feeling this new Inspector is a lot more than he appears'

Mohammed frowned. That was not good news. Cogan was the only agent in the area. If he was compromised the CIA would lose a valued asset.

'Did you say you had been accompanied all the time I was away' he asked suddenly.

'More or less. They escorted me to a canteen. Given coffee and sandwiches as well. Quite friendly really'

'So, you were away from the helicopter most of the time'

'Except for a system check and a re-fuel; yes'

Mohammed didn't talk for a while as he thought through what was bugging him. When it did he tapped Cogan on the arm.

'We need to land. ***NOW***'

He pointed to the thick vegetation below 'you have to be kidding. I could circle around for hours and not find a clearing'

'Are we on the airports radar yet' he shouted trying to think.

'In about two minutes. What's the problem partner'

'If we lose altitude will it keep us off the radar?' he asked thinking out loud.

'It's been a while since I flew at tree-top height, it will, at least until we get a lot closer'

The last time he did this was as a pilot with a payload of US Rangers aboard Cogan recalled. The danger was. A flock of birds ascending from the trees below could down a machine just as effectively as a SAM missile.

Mohammed grabbed the map from its concealed drawer under the seat. He plotted a course for the airport. He found what he was looking for and tapped the pilot on the shoulder.

'What is this!' he asked stabbing his finger on the map.

Cogan looked at it and grinned ***'your landing site partner'***

THE AIRPORT

The NH-90 landed only ten minutes behind schedule.

Cogan powered down the machine. Orange flashing lights suddenly filled the cockpit as Police cars surrounded the helicopter.

The pilot ignored the commotion and went around to help his passenger out.

The *Inspector* approached and bowed politely 'I trust you had a good trip Mister Cogan'

'Hi Inspector. It looks like you've got a promotion' he smiled; nodding in the direction of the armed police officers surrounding them.

'Sadly, the criminal elements sometimes use force. A precaution only, I assure you'

'What's all this about Mister Cogan. I've had enough excitement to last me a year. I need to be away to my hotel' Mohammed asked angrily.

'Mister Suleiman' the Inspector said looking his way 'I have been informed of the attack on your vehicle. Rest assured the culprits will be found and dealt with. Your quick thinking probably saved the Major's life. He is recovering from his ordeal by the way. When I have concluded my business here we will escort you to your hotel'

'*Via a **Police Cell** I bet*' Mohammed thought; taking a dislike to the smug looking Inspector.

'**_Search the helicopter_**' he shouted to his men.

They made a show of searching the inside; then unhooked the lever securing the door to the luggage compartment.

The Inspector waited. His speech was ready.

The man searching the compartment leaned inside and rummaged around. He looked at the Inspector and shook his head.

The smug smile disappeared '**_search again_**' he ordered.

The man again shook his head and shrugged.

The Inspector controlled his anger long enough to apologize for the delay. Swiveling on his heels he walked quickly back to the waiting police car. Two minutes later the landing pad was empty of policeman.

'How did you know I was being set up Mohammed' Cogan asked.

'Just a guess Cogan'

'I owe you partner'

'Just doing my job Cogan. The Agency would be very upset at losing their only asset in Mandalay. I don't think I'm getting that lift to the hotel' he finished.

Cogan laughed heartily at that 'do you want me to drop you off?'

'No. The message I asked you to send the Captain of the Learjet was for him to file a flight plan. I cannot chance getting arrested or searched. You need to watch that Inspector from now on. I have a feeling he doesn't like being made a fool of!'

EARLIER

The Buddhist Temple lay perched on top of a huge limestone outcropping. It rose from the jungle below. Access to the Temple was via a crude lift. Or a *helicopter*!

Cogan hovered over the building making sure the patio below would support the helicopters weight. He expertly dropped the machine onto the mosaic tiles keeping the blades turning at maximum.

Mohammed jumped out and ran to the rear. Opening the luggage compartment, he pulled out a package the size of a shoe box. Slitting open the package with his knife he tasted the white powder. He then angrily tossed the entire contents over a wall.

Getting back in; he gave the thumbs up to Cogan.

The whole exercise had taken no more than five minutes.

CHAPTER 7
DISTRACTIONS

Mohammed thanked the Stewardess for the drinks and the sandwich. It had been many hours since he had last eaten. He glanced out of the Learjet window but he wasn't admiring the landscape below. Since boarding the plane his mind had been pre-occupied with the events of the past forty-eight hours.

Something didn't add up; but until he studied the photographs he wasn't going to assume anything. What I need to do is compare what was there in the past he decided.

He pulled on some headphones 'I need to speak to Langley; Captain'

The call was put through 'Hello Michael. We got the message from Cogan you had departed from Mandalay. Do you need flights booking to come home?'

'Not yet Katherine, I want to study the photographs I've taken before I make any decisions. Can you get me satellite images of the area around the compound and the valley beyond? I need to compare them to the shots I have taken'

'I think that can be arranged. I don't know how long it will take though! This mission is not categorized as urgent any more. Where are planning to land?'

'That's why I'm calling. I need a large screen to overlay the images. It will probably need someone who knows what they're doing as well. Any ideas?'

Katherine took a few moments to consider his request 'the nearest base is Kuwait but what you are asking for is an Imaging Specialist. I'm not sure one is available in Kuwait'

'I don't want to hang around for days until one turns up. What about our Base in Spain?'

'You mean Rota? They will have one there for sure but I'll call them just to be certain'

'Get back to me to confirm. I'll check with the Captain it's not a problem'

'It's no problem Sir' the Captain confirmed but it will mean a re-fuel along the route 'the Learjet Sixty has a maximum range of just over four thousand four hundred miles. Rota is well over that distance and we have a head wind'

I understand Captain but I don't want to go directly to the Base. File a flight plan for Seville in Spain. My cover is still intact for now. I don't want to chance anybody checking up on where I'm going. In fact, a couple of days in a friendly city won't do me any harm' he decided.

SEVILLE; SPAIN

'Legend has it that Seville was founded by Hercules. It has its origins linked with the Tartessian civilization. Under the Romans it was called Hispalis. The Moors called it Isbiliya. However, its high point came after the discovery of America' the Tour Guide informed her group as they stood admiring the **Cathedral La Giralda's** minarets.

Khan had booked into the hotel in the Centre of Seville under his real name.

It was time to shed the disguise.

Having left all his clothes in Mandalay he decided to do some shopping.

He had joined the tour on an impulse. He needed a distraction. The sightseeing tour was perfect.

'Are you enjoying the tour sir' the guide asked disturbing his daydreaming.

'Sorry I was miles away' he replied turning around 'and yes I am. Your City is **muy hermoso** Senorita' impressing her with his limited Spanish.

'Why thank you Senor. Your Spanish is excellent'

'You were about to add; for an **American** that is' he teased.

She gave him a little pout understanding the remark was intended to fluster her.

'Are you staying in Seville long?'

'Two days only I'm afraid. Can you recommend a good restaurant by the way?' he asked feeling guilty at teasing her.

'My uncle has the best restaurant in the whole of Andalucía' she boasted proudly 'I will give you directions'

'Or you could *join* me?'

The guide studied him for a few moments. It wasn't the first time a visitor had hit on her and she would have passed the remark off with a *'no thank you.'*

The American had piqued her interest. There was **something** about him.

'I would love to Senor.......?'

'My name is Michael Khan and as you can tell; I'm American; from New York. Shall we say seven o'clock Senorita ....?'

'My name is Maria; and I will collect you at your hotel at seven' she confirmed moving away to join her other charges.

Maria duly arrived at seven.

Michael had to do a double take and keep his mouth closed at the sight that greeted him.

Maria had shed her smart tour guide uniform. It was replaced by what he later learned was a typical Feria Dress.

'The Feria de Abril starts tonight Michael' she told him. Secretly pleased with the effect she was having 'every woman; young and old; will be wearing a dress like this one. It may interest you that no two dresses are the same'

She was stunning. The dress hugged her slim waist. It was cut low to reveal a full bosom. Maria did a twirl. The effect was dazzling.

Michael had wanted a distraction but this was more than he could have imagined.

The restaurant was located near the Port. They decided to walk. The night was warm, the sky clear. In summer the temperatures reached over forty degrees he was informed.

The restaurant was packed with diners. Without Maria reserving a table he would not have been able to eat there. He had been introduced to the Uncle; and got a stern behave yourself look.

Their table was situated at the end of a long terrace. Maria had ordered Sangria 'but a little different from what the tourist get' she told him. A little guiltily at revealing that information.

Michael was not a drinker of alcohol but the Sangria was filled with fruit. He casually stirred the jug lost in thought.

'I think it is ready to drink Senor Khan' she said smiling and shaking him from his reverie.

'I'm sorry Maria my mind was elsewhere' he apologized pouring two large glasses of Sangria.

It really was excellent.

A breeze blew down the terrace blowing napkins onto the tiled floor. The smell of Jasmin followed; making Michael breath in deeply. It brought back memories of a village in Africa.

'It does that quite often late in the evening. It is because we are close to the river. The Port has a fascinating history. Many famous explorers have started their expeditions from there. Ferdinand Magellan is probably my favorite explorer I think. Did you know he was the first to circumnavigate the earth?'

'Didn't he come to a sticky end?' he asked remembering a little of his history lessons.

'You could say that. A native Chief called Mactan defeated the raiding party after they landed on his Island. The transcripts from the period explained the Captain was cut down by *bamboo spears and crude cutlasses* as he made sure his crew where safely in the boats'

'He was a very brave man if that was the case'

'His body was never recovered did you know that? He had no wife and family either so it seemed his existence would be lost forever'

'You seem to love your job Maria. Not everybody is so fortunate' he told her loudly.

The Spanish diners deemed it necessary to *shout!*

'I studied history at college. The tour guide position was intended as a temporary job' she laughed flashing perfectly white teeth.

'History and what happened in the past is important' he answered.

Maria was about to reply but the look that had come over his face stopped her.

'Is there something wrong Michael' she asked concerned.

Khan didn't answer for a moment.

The knot in his stomach had returned. The feeling of well-being had disappeared. He shouldn't be here.

He would leave for Rota the first thing in the morning.

'My apologies Maria. This has been a wonderful evening but it is time for me to leave. Can I escort you home?'

'That is not necessary. I live close by. What is the problem Michael?' she asked now convinced there was something troubling him.

'It is nothing to concern yourself with and I apologize again for my mood. There is a village in Asia that needs my help and this **distraction** is delaying that help'

She wanted to know more but had the feeling further information would not be forthcoming. This man had depth. She had never met anyone like him before.

He stood up to leave.

She stood as well and grabbed his arm to stop him leaving.

'I have changed my mind Michael. I want you to escort me home'

CHAPTER 8

LANGLEY

Katherine Carter welcomed her visitor. Just like Michael Khan she decided her photo didn't do her justice.   Even in a smart business suit she looked amazing.

Sunita Win thanked the CIA Agent for seeing her.

'No thanks needed Agent Win.   I understand you have an appointment with my Director'

'Please call me Sunita; and it is just Miss Win for now.   Director Wyden resigned yesterday.   I couldn't see myself working under his replacement'

'He is a good man Sunita. It took courage to ask for help. That didn't go down well with the Defense Department'

'The thought of losing his step-daughter clouded his judgement. We had a long talk yesterday. He updated me on everything that has happened by the way. Where is **_Agent Khan?_**'

It was a blunt question designed to catch the woman off-guard. It nearly worked.

'You know I can't tell you that Sunita'

'Your Director is going to offer me a position with the CIA.   I will accept on the condition I can follow up on the situation in Myanmar.   I don't like leaving things half finished. Are you and Michael very **_close_**?'

Katherine dropped her eyes.   Even the mention of his name brought a reaction.

'I see' Sunita said not waiting for an answer

Katherine studied her visitor 'I can see why Michael was impressed with you Sunita' she answered 'he mentioned you more than once'

'Touché Katherine. Now we understand each other let us be friends. I only wish to know about this man. We both know he is special'

Katherine came to a decision. If Michael was about to get involved in the situation in Myanmar, he would need help. If nothing else; with speaking the local language.

'His name is Michael Khan but he took the name Mohammed when he moved to North Africa. He had been stationed in Egypt to uncover a terrorist cell. It was six months before he got a breakthrough. We still don't know how he did it because shortly after that he resigned as an Agent. The next thing I knew he had married a local woman. His son was born shortly after'

'He has a ***family?*** Sunita asked surprised.

'His wife and son were killed in an attack on their village'

'That's sad' Sunita replied genuinely sorry for his loss.

'He stayed in the country to help the people gain Independence from the Government. I think he already knew it was a battle they couldn't win. The town he was in held out for weeks while the UN tried to arrange a ceasefire and open negotiations but they failed'

Sunita sat upright 'you're not talking about that town in North Africa that was on the news. Didn't a Private Jet make an emergency landing slap in the middle of a civil war'

'What happened over the next twenty-four hours would take some believing. The English football player and the French Stewardess did their part in bringing the situation to the attention of the media'

'I have a feeling there is a **but** coming' Sunita said.

Kathline nodded 'Michael e-mailed me. He wanted background information on one of the passengers. The man turned out to be one of the most important Arms Dealer in Asia. I was a second away from ending my career. As it happened I needn't have worried'

Sunita digested the information.

'Khan blackmailed the Arms Dealer, didn't he?'

'He did. But what information he had on him; he wouldn't reveal to us'

'I remember watching the Englishman; emerging from the hotel basement with all those children around him. It was quite moving'

'The passengers and the crew believed Michael and the Arms Dealer where killed when the shells hit the building. He would prefer to keep it that way Sunita'

She nodded in understanding.

Khan had arranged a video call in less than one hour. She picked up the telephone and called her Directors office.

After a few minutes, she looked at Sunita *'are you in'* she asked bluntly.

Sunita nodded a yes.

Katherine replaced the receiver 'a **Contract** will be with you in ten minutes. Sign it and you can join me in Operations. I assume you want to **know** where Michael is?'

CHAPTER 9

ROTA AIR BASE; SPAIN

It had been a few years since Khan had been in an Operations Room. The CIA Technician had done his best to explain all the new computer programs. The photographs he had taken were now over-laid with satellite images from years past.

It was impressive technology.

The computer had scanned the images and was now highlighting areas of interest.

Katherine suddenly appeared in a box on the screen 'what are you looking for Michael' she asked him.

'Hi Katherine. The dealer in Egypt showed me a decent sized gem. I couldn't place its origin. He hinted there was more where that came from. I was expecting to see multiple mine workings'

'What is that structure perched on the hillside' she asked highlighting it on the screen 'it looks new. A laboratory of some kind you think?'

'**That must be the place Doctor Robson mentioned**' someone said in the background.

'**Sunita!** What are you doing at Langley?' asked a surprised Khan.

She poked her head in front of the camera 'it is nice to see you as well **Michael Khan**!'

'Sunita has joined the Agency. Ex-Director Wyden sends his regards by the way. He is in your debt'

'I'm glad it all turned out OK'

'What are we looking for Michael?' Katherine asked.

'What you need to ask ourselves is; where are the **villagers**'

There were multiple dwellings placed haphazardly across the valley. Typical of a displaced community attempting to establish a place to live.

'There are no people' Katherine suddenly realized.

'There are signs of recent occupation. The Muslim refugees who occupied it have all been removed however. There is a news item you should see' he said nodding to the technician beside him.

NEWS ITEM:

BURMA ACCUSED OF GENOCIDE

Military operations in Myanmar formally Burma have caused thousands to flee across the border to Bangladesh. A UN official said the local Muslim community in Burma were being ethnically cleansed; alleging that government soldiers have killed and raped civilians.

'Oh, my god is that still going on?' Katherine gasped 'surely the UN can put a stop to it'

'Don't hold your breath Katherine' Khan angrily replied.

'I'm sorry Michael but that doesn't add up' Sunita said putting her head in front of the camera again.

'What do you mean?' he asked.

'Why bother to kidnap a Doctor to heal the cholera victims if you wanted to get rid of them?'

'You have a point' he conceded 'what's *your* theory?'

'That structure on the hillside. What's going on in there? You have already mentioned the lack of mine workings associated with extracting diamonds. If that's the case what's that large excavation in the background. Why kidnap then hire the Professor to survey the area. His brief was to locate the best site for a small airstrip and access road. Why not just hire someone legitimately? The only reason I can think of is they didn't want anyone knowing about it. Killing the Professor made sure of that'

'But how did they know he was going to be there' Khan asked.

A chill went down his spine. He was thinking the unthinkable.

Katherine broke his train of thought 'I suggest we discuss that later; on a secure line. For now; let's finish this assessment'

Sunita had gone silent as well. Things that had happened in the past suddenly becoming clear.

'My expertise only extends to Diamonds or Jade mines. The excavation in the background doesn't fit that type of operation' Khan stated annoyed he couldn't come up with an explanation.

'Excuse me sir. Maybe I can help' the Technician suggested.

'Go ahead'

'I have made comparisons with similar workings. You are correct in saying this is not the kind of mining associated with diamond extraction'

'Then what type is it associated with?' he asked.

'It is like mines extracting ***URANIUM*** he replied 'it is possible they discovered diamonds as well but not likely. Let me provide more background information'

The technician imputed a news item on the screen:

Three operating configurations

To extract uranium, it is necessary to access the deposit. This is done by:

- *removing the rock covering shallow deposits lying at a depth of less than 150 meters, in the case of **open-pit mining**,*
- *penetrating tunnels where the ore is located at a depth, as is the case with **underground mines**,*
- *by borehole mining, involving the injection of a leaching solution into the deposit to dissolve the uranium. The production solution that solubilized the uranium is then pumped out to extract the uranium. This is known as in-situ recovery. This method is used for low-grade deposits located in sandy layers between impermeable clay layers. The only deposit mined in this way is in Kazakhstan.*

*Open-pit uranium mines offer the advantage of **easy access to the ore**: the techniques and machinery used are like those used in quarries or on public works sites.*

*These mines can reach a depth of **several hundred meters**.*

'There is an additional item you should see as well sir' the Technician added.

*The operation of uranium mines can present **health risks for miners** through the inhalation of **radon**, a rare gas produced through the disintegration of uranium, along with dust.*

Khan's mind was working furiously trying to solve the puzzle. He was missing something. When the answer came he just smiled. It was so obvious!

'Katherine. I have been looking at this all wrong. What the Technician has just said makes complete sense. There has been ethnic cleansing in the north but this area is not controlled just by the Military. There is no way they can finance an operation as complicated as this. Someone or some organisation is bank rolling it. The diamond mining is a cover. It also helps in laundering ***Blood Diamonds***'

'If you're right; this operation could launder millions of dollars in illegal gems'

'Not millions Katherine but billions. The illegal sale of blood diamonds has produced billions of dollars to fund civil wars and other conflicts in various African nations. Sierra Leone; Angola and Liberia to name but a few. The people behind these civil wars and rebellions; oppose legitimate governments and want control over the area's diamond industry'

'Do you think the military could be involved in organizing a Coupe? The country has only just elected a civilian government' Sunita asked concerned.

'It is a possibility but not likely. The military still have effective control over security so why bother. They still get away with human rights abuses. The UN hasn't managed to stop that either'

'I get the impression the UN is not on your Christmas list Michael' Sunita said 'Oh sorry just remembered you don't do that as a Muslim' apologizing.

'Believe it or not we used to have a tree in our house during the holiday. My father liked to invite his friends around for a drink. He has a real liking for egg nog' he laughed.

The two women laughed as well; happy the tension building up had been released.

Katherine became serious 'all this is speculation. I cannot approach the Director unless we have hard evidence diamonds are being laundered. I feel for the civilians caught up in all this but again how can we help them. The UN can't even stop the ethnic cleansing in the North of the country. The mining is also speculation but if they have uncovered Uranium the US will want to know where it's being processed and who is the intended buyer'

'Which will all take time and cost lives Katherine. The only way to be certain of our facts is for me to see for myself'

'And for me to come with you Mister Khan and don't even think about arguing' Sunita told him firmly.

Khan smiled at her fortitude 'I think your new boss will have something to say about that' he said understanding she had joined the Agency.

He waited until Katherine was back in view 'I will let you ask the questions. Get back to me later when you know for sure' he said cutting the link.

Katherine jotted something on a note pad 'bring it to me as soon as you have the information' she told the Technician.

Sunita followed Katherine back to her office.

'You are not going to Myanmar Sunita' she stated flatly.

'But Katherine. Khan needs me to interpret the language'

'You do not have the experience or the training'

'Maybe I should speak to the Director' she replied instantly regretting the comment.

The icy stare made the woman opposite gulp 'if you ever try to blackmail or coerce me again **_Agent Win_** I will see to it that you are washing cells out in Guantanamo Bay. Do we understand each other?'

'I'm sorry Katherine that was uncalled for. I wish to help Khan that's all'

She hated to admit it but Sunita was correct. Having someone who understood and spoke the language was a benefit. She would consider it but first she needed answers.

'When Wyden came to us he produced dossiers on the Professor and his step-daughter. He did not however provide background information on you, suggesting it was not relevant. How long were you with the Defense Department?'

'Almost a year; but not as a Field Agent. I have a Doctorate in Languages. I am fluent in five languages and understand another three or four. They made me section head in less than six months. The offer to accompany the Professor came directly from Assistant Director Wyden himself. It was all very hush hush but he explained it was just a baby-sitting job no more. He never expected anything to happen'

'Wyden was your Handler. Was he the only one who knew what you were doing?'

Sunita frowned at the question 'come to think of it he was. What's going on Katherine?' she asked confused.

The Technician entered and placed a file on the desk.

Katherine nodded her thanks and opened it. She read the contents and then angrily slapped the file on the desk.

'***Son-of-a-bitch***' she growled 'tell me what you knew about the Professor; don't miss anything out'

She did as request.

She waited until Sunita finished.

'You had no idea the Professor was also a renowned authority on mining for Uranium.

The man has published articles on the subject'

'My god, no I didn't' she answered now understanding what Katherine was getting at.

She had been used. The whole thing was a set up to get the Professor into Myanmar.

'Why not just hire him?'

'I can only guess at that. How Wyden's involved I don't yet know. He wanted you to keep track of the Professors' movements that's for sure. I think the kidnapping made him re-assess the situation. I don't think the kidnappers; if we can still call them that; knew it was his step-daughter. He couldn't go to his Director and ask for help. Too many questions would be asked and he couldn't contact these people in Myanmar so he came to us. My Director is not going to like an old friend using him this way'

'But we could have been killed' she said angrily.

'Possible but I don't think so. At least not while you were in Myanmar. Your death would have been investigated. The Professor however had to go. He knew too much!'

'My god! He would have tried to kill me when I arrived back in the US. An accident of some kind' she said angry now.

'When Michael put you on that plane it interfered with his plans. I bet he's been keeping you well away from the Department since you landed'

'He asked me to stay away until he could file a report. He suggested my handling of the situation could be called into question. That's when I decided to call you. Michael gave me your number before I left'

'We would have contacted him eventually as a matter of courtesy. I bet if we called the Department we would be told you were on sick leave'

'I was about to ask; what was Wyden getting out of doing this; but I think Michael has already supplied the answer' Sunita said.

Katherine tapped a pen on the desk. It was something she did when thinking things through.

'What is Wyden going to do now he's resigned' she asked.

'He mentioned organizing his father's campaign'

'I thought he was already a Senator' she said trying to remember Wyden's family background.

'He is. I'm talking about his **Presidential** campaign'

'**Jesus!** That's why he's doing all this. Running for President costs a lot of money. It helps if you're a billionaire like our current one'

Sunita suddenly jumped in her seat 'Oh my god I've just remembered he's invited me to lunch tomorrow. He wanted to show his gratitude for helping his step-daughter. I was going to cancel. If I was on my way to Spain that is!' she asked questioningly.

'I will make you a deal Sunita. Wear a wire to this lunch tomorrow and you will be on the next plane to Rota'

It was a no brainer!

A RESTAURANT: DOWTOWN MANHATTEN

Anyone requesting a table at the door would be politely told all the tables were reserved today. They would get the same response tomorrow; and the day after. If you had to ask; you were not one of the elite and privileged.

The head waiter at the entrance checked her identity and signaled a waiter.

Wyden was already at the table 'Sunita! I'm glad you could make it. Please check out the menu and order whatever you want'

She did; noting there were no prices anywhere on the menu. If you had to ask the table would suddenly be reserved the next time you called.

'I would like to thank you again for seeing my step-daughter home. It is because of her I resigned. She was never happy with my career choice. She didn't actually say *blood on my hands* but I got the message'

For a moment, she thought he was referring to the Professor. His death had already been accredited to over-indulgence!

'She is a very brave woman Mister Wyden. It sounds funny not calling you Director any more'

'You had a promising career. I'm sorry I couldn't stop the investigation into your handling of the affair. The Department will be in contact very soon but as you have already resigned I see no point in them taking things further. What will you do now?'

'I have a Doctorate in Languages. Any university will be more than happy to offer me a position. Not here in New York though. I was thinking of moving to Canada'

A little over the top Katherine thought; listening to the conversation.

'Well I wish you all the best'

'Please excuse me. I need to visit the bathroom' she said getting up.

A waiter was already pulling her chair back.

Wyden flicked the cover off his cell phone 'forget the surveillance. She's planning to leave the country' he told the person at the end of the call 'I want no more **accidents**. Is that understood or our deal is off. Keep the bug in her apartment if you must but that is all!' he finished slamming the cover angrily.

Sunita returned and thanked him for a lovely meal. She collected her handbag from off the seat and left.

A taxi pulled up to the curb as she left the restaurant.

'How was I' she asked her purse.

'The microphone worked perfectly. Wyden called someone while you were away. We are tracing the call now. Be careful at home. Your apartment is bugged'

'I just need to pack a bag then I'm gone!'

Spain and Michael Khan. Here I come!

CHAPTER 10

A RESTAURANT: ABU DABI

Tabarrok Shabbat stood up from the table to meet his dinner guests.

He bowed politely and extended his hand in greeting.

'Welcome Mohammed Khan. My house is your house' he said in greeting.

'You are most gracious Tabarrok. May I introduce Sunita Win'

'You have a knack of attracting beautiful woman Mister Khan' he said bowing graciously.

'Thank you for the compliment Mister Tabarrok. The view from the restaurant's terrace is quite amazing' Sunita replied; **in his native tongue**.

The look of surprise was written all over his face.

He burst out laughing 'and still full of surprises I see! Please join me at my table. Order whatever you wish. You are my guests this evening'

The talk was kept to matters concerning the world at large until the meal had finished.

 It was time to talk business.

'I will understand if you do not wish to answer my question *Tabarrok Shabbat.* But I must ask it. Do you know what is going on in Myanmar'?

'Are you referring to the shipment of Arms to the Military or the ethnic cleansing of our brothers'

'Your business is no concern of mine but it would be helpful in knowing you have connections in this country. The abuse of Muslims and their displacement will wait another day'

Tabarrok Shabbat studied his guest and made a decision 'I am in your debt Mohammed Khan. How can I be of service?'

'We need to enter Myanmar discreetly'

'Cannot your CIA help you in this matter' he asked.

'I would prefer not to involve them. What I'm about to attempt is all my own idea. I will also need a very special type of explosive'

Shabbat considered his request 'There are no deliveries due until next year but it may be time for me to visit the Capital to see old friends. Maybe I can **drop you off** on the way?'

Mohammed smiled 'that sounds like an excellent idea' Sunita waited until Shabbat left the restaurant before asking the question 'How is he going to drop us of Michael. I thought there were no airports in that area and we can't go to Mandalay again surely!'

'I agree but I meant **drop** us off literally'

'Oh hell! You don't really mean a parachute drop. Michael I have never done anything like that before' she told him a little frightened.

'Don't worry. You will not be needing a parachute of your own'

She was about to ask many questions but the grin on his face stopped her 'why do I have a feeling I'm not going to like this'

THE HOTEL

Michael and Sunita returned to the hotel keeping up the pretense they were a honeymoon couple. It would take two days for Shabbat to organize the delivery to Myanmar. They may as well enjoy the time by sightseeing they decided.

Michael had been the perfect gentleman much to Sunita's annoyance. The close proximity to such a man as Michael Khan had triggered her imagination to what could be.

She had tried to discuss his time in North Africa. He had politely moved the conversation to another subject.

It was their last night. They would be collected early in the morning.

Khan had showered first as usual to allow her to use the large bath at her leisure.

'Make the most of it Sunita. It's unlikely we will get the chance to wash for the next few days' he said; trying his best not to admire the way the robe hugged her damp body.

She finished drying her hair with the towel and bent low to shake it lose.

Her robe fell open. She stood up making no move to cover her nakedness.

The invitation was obvious.

Khan sighed deeply at the sight and came over to her.

He pulled the robe together and politely tied the belt *'**when this is over**'* was all he said.

CHAPTER 11
THE RETURN

They had caught a flight to Ben Galuru International Airport in India the next day.

Shabbat had met them at the terminal and escorted the pair to his Private aircraft.

'The AAC Angel is a turbo-prop aircraft with a range of one thousand seven hundred nautical miles. Mandalay is well within its maximum range but we will need to chart a route that takes us close to Bangladesh. We will contact the Control Tower as we get closer explaining we had strong headwinds. Nothing unusual over the Bay of Bengal' he advised them.

'Have you managed to acquire everything I asked for?' Khan asked.

'The rifle was no problem including the specialist night scope. The Bandolier Explosive was a little harder to acquire. I don't suppose you're going to explain why you need such a specific explosive?'

He told him.

'May Allah, be with you Mohammed Khan for you will surely need his protection' he said shaking his head. Sunita had been reserved since the night before. She had understood Khan's reluctance to get involved with a woman he would be placing in danger.

'I need to focus' he had explained and 'not make decisions based on personal feelings'

She had understood; but that didn't stop the erotic dreams continuing.

Today however she had a different feeling. Fear!

'What the hell is **_Tandem Skydiving_** Khan' she had asked suspiciously.

'It means we will be harnessed together. All you have to do is enjoy the freefall'

She wasn't convinced; and even less as the Angel's side door opened.

She made the mistake of looking down.

Khan felt her grab his arm.

Shabbat turned around from the flight console and put his thumb in the air.

Khan tapped her on the shoulder to distract her.

She was about ask something but it turned into a **_scream_** as they tumbled out of the door; dragging a bundle with them.

Sunita's fear was gradually replaced by awe as the silence engulfed them.

The wind buffeted her cheeks. She tried to remember his instructions to her and stretched her arms and legs out wide. Khan put a thumb up to her goggles to say well done.

It was an incredible sensation. Why hadn't she done this sooner?

She gazed down at the lush green landscape below. It was a wonderful sight.

But it was getting closer.

A lot closer!

The opening of the canopy forced her body into the harness. She gasped as the air went from her lungs but remembered her instructions. Khan toggled the ropes as they came into land. At the last moment, they lifted back into the air then landed softly.

Quickly cutting away the parachute he unhooked Sunita and began pulling in the flapping chute. It would be covered under rocks. He collected the three bags that had been attached to his feet on the descent.

Sunita had already discarded her suit in favor of jungle fatigues.

'That wasn't too bad' he said smiling at her appearance.

He wasn't expecting the response.

She flung her arms around his neck and kissed him 'promise me, we will do that again' she said breathlessly.

THE TOWER COMPOUND

The Barret M96 rested easily on Khan's legs. The tri-pod had been assembled. Khan would mount the weapon only at the last moment. They had reached a small hill near the compound unseen but he wasn't going to take any chances at being spotted. If that happened they would disappear into the undergrowth and seek shelter until the danger had passed.

It was late afternoon. The sun was at their backs. The Sniper Rifle had a maximum range of one thousand eight hundred meters. The compound was just over one thousand five hundred. The distance to the box mounted on the Control Tower however was two hundred meters further on.

During his time at Rota Airbase he had asked the Technician to produce a 3-D image of the line of sight. The computers had done their wizardry. As he looked through his scope he was astounded at the accuracy of the programmer. He had even included the swaying palm trees occasionally dancing across his vision.

It was time.

Khan slid back the bolt and inserted the point fifty caliber bullet.

'Are you ready Sunita?' he asked, the almost immobile woman beside him.

She just nodded and looked once again at the tower in the distance. She had utmost faith in Khan's abilities but this was taking some believing. She had even been allowed to gaze down the ten-X Telescopic sight and still had been unable to identify the box in question.

'We need to wait until the sun is at the correct angle' he had told her in answer to her questions. He had explained but she still wasn't convinced.

'If I'm successful we need to reach the clearing in less than twenty minutes. Cogan has assured me he can reach us by then. The sun will be behind the escarpment as we fly in.

I only hope the villagers are all together in one place. Whatever happens you need to be well away from that village when I set the charges'

Khan settled into his firing position. He controlled his breathing. It was always the same. Images of the past flashed through his mind. He ignored the doubts and the self-recrimination. He had long ago come to terms with the death and destruction his weapon could inflict.

He pulled the trigger.

Sunita watched fascinated as he ignored the bullets flight. In less than a second another bullet was in the chamber.

Khan **had** watched the impact.

A guard stationed below the tower heard a clang as the bullet struck a metal support. He shrugged and ignored it. The lack of interest would cost him his life.

Khan adjusted his sights. The strobe light emitting from the box was invisible accept through a scope such as was mounted on the Barret M96. It was also only visible at certain times of the day.

Khan pulled the trigger.

The HMX material; *also, known as octogen or cyclotetramethylene-tetranitramine; is a powerful and relatively insensitive nitroamine high explosive. It is used almost exclusively in military applications. It is currently considered a state-of-the-art military explosive.*

The explosion ripped one metal strut into lethal flying shards. The next strut buckled under the concussion. Khan watched in fascination then concern as the tower still stood upright. It was only a matter of time.

The opposing struts gave up their efforts to support the tower above. It toppled sideways. Onto a building below.

The building stored Ordnance. The smoldering metal girders sliced the corrugated warehouse in two. The ammunition stored caught fire in seconds. The ensuing explosions ripped the rest of the compound to shreds. The guard was already dead.

'**_My God_**!' cried Sunita as she watched the chaos unfold.

Khan was already pulling her away and talking into a radio 'we need to go. **_NOW_**'

Cogan brought the helicopter in low to avoid detection. Within seconds of collecting his passengers he was airborne and heading for the village in the distance. He glanced quickly at the glow in the distance and winked at his passenger.

'So far so good' he said to himself.

CHAPTER 12
THE VILLAGE

The old man poked the open fire then spat into it; then grabbed his ribs as the pain returned. The beating he had received from the African guards had been brutal. Fighting them had been stupid but what else could he do. The men had selected his two daughters as their playthings for the night. He had argued. Pleaded. And then attacked them. The pleas for mercy from his children had been ignored until the eldest had promised they would do anything the men desired.

Men and women came to offer their sympathy but nothing else.

He pushed them away; disgusted by their weakness and ashamed of his own.

He gazed up the hillside to the dam in the distance; and to the compound beyond.

He spat once more into the fire; then shielded his eyes as the downdraft from the **helicopters** rotary blades scattered embers in all directions. He stood erect determined not to show fear at whatever was about to happen.

The helicopter took off again and disappeared towards the dam.

A woman approached and spoke in his own language **'please take me to your Head Man'** she begged.

He was confused unsure what to do or say. The young woman spoke with authority and purpose!

She spoke again *'we must evacuate your people from this valley. The dam is going to be destroyed. Everything you see will be washed away!'*

The woman meant everything she was saying.

'Come with me' he told her.

The Head Man was not convinced.

'How could such a thing happen' he laughed dismissively.

'Because **Mohammed Khan** said it will be' she told him calmly 'the same **Mohammed Khan** who stopped the forces of evil destroying his village in North Africa. The same **Mohammed Khan** who no more the thirty minutes ago; destroyed the Compound over the hill' she said pointing to the glow in the distance.

They had all heard the booms and whistles of the ammunition exploding but had no idea what had happened. The Head Man looked once more at the woman.

He banged the pole he was carrying on the ground three times.

It was the signal that their Leader had important news!

'Take only what you need for a short journey. Tell everyone to make their way up the paths to the hills above the dam. We leave this accursed place now' he shouted to the village Elders.

Sunita sighed in relief.

'One more thing Chief. Khan wishes you to **torch the village** as you leave!'

'I would like to meet this ***Profit of Doom*** when this is over woman' he told her.

THE DAM

Cogan brought the helicopter in front of the dam and spoke to Khan on his headset 'when we clear the top of the dam there will be a strong wind'

The helicopter bucked and yawned as it cleared the wall surrounding the dam. A road wide enough to take a single vehicle ran the full length of the dam and disappeared into the hillside. It was empty of traffic.

'So far so good' Cogan thought again.

'Can you put me down on top of that tower' Khan shouted

The tower was a square structure two thirds of a way along the dam's roadway. It was the entrance to the dams' interior.

Cogan tried all he could but admitted defeat 'I could land on the parapet but any sudden gust of wind would throw us off again. I don't fancy your chances of surviving that fall' he said pointing to the chasm below.

'I'll drop down by guy rope. The packages can go first'

Cogan didn't like that idea one bit but agreed. Time was moving on. He was surprised the compound on the hill had not decided to investigate the disturbance in the distance!

Khan pushed himself out of the door and waited. If he misjudged the drop he would go tumbling over the towers side. He would not survive the fall.

He let go and abseiled down.

Unhooking he dropped to the roofs stone floor and waited for Cogan to fly away.

'Good luck partner' the Pilot shouted in his earpiece as he banked the helicopter away. Khan wasted no time. He left the bag containing his sniper rifle on the roof but dropped the second one over the parapet and onto the road below. It thumped heavily onto the tarmac. He climbed down the metal ladder and examined the heavily padlocked door. This was no time for delays.

Packing gelignite at strategic points around the door he stepped back and said to himself **_fire in the hole_**

The door buckled and collapsed inwards.

Khan kicked it aside and made his way into the dams' interior.

Down he went, thankful the emergency lighting was sufficient to light his way.

He reached the bottom. Out of breath from carrying the heavy satchel.

He was no expert but his years as Marine and then as a CIA Agent had taught him many things. Demolishing a dam was not one of them however. He had taken advice from an old friend but one look at the dam wall made him understand his fears were unfounded.

The Contractor who had built the dam wall had made a fortune; by using **_inferior materials._**

A crack had already appeared in the concrete. No water was seeping through but it was only a matter of time before urgent repairs were needed to prevent the structure from collapsing.

Khan readjusted his planned siting of the Explosive packed in Tubes. He placed the first one under the crack. He then moved along the walkway placing the rest as he went.

Satisfied he looked at his watch.

Sunita should have by now evacuated the village. He flipped open a plastic cover and pressed a switch to arm the detonators. The countdown had begun. Even if the guards in the compound realized what was happening there would be no time to get to the base and disarm the explosive.

It was time to go.

THE COMPOUND

The African General pushed the woman aside and climbed out of bed determined to shoot the man responsible for disturbing his enjoyment. He grabbed a bottle of Bourbon on the way to the door and drank a large measure. He flung open the door 'I will feed your carcass to my lions back home if this is not important'

The soldier ignored the state of his Commander 'General; there are fires being lit down in the village' he informed him stiffly.

'Fires!' Why would I be interested in these fucking stupid villagers and their cooking arrangements' he bawled.

'No Sir. I mean the huts themselves are on fire'

This was interesting but was it important enough to leave the little woman in his bed.

'Contact the Base and tell them what's happening. They can send a helicopter to investigate' he decided thinking his duty had been done.

'They do not answer General' the soldier informed him.

It took a few moments for that to register 'are they having communication problems?'

'I do not think so General. We have been unable to raise them ever since the light in the sky'

He pushed the soldier aside and went outside. Sure, enough a glow could be seen over the hillside. He walked further into the compounds square. A light in the distance caught his eye. He walked over to the fence and peered down into the darkness below. The light appeared again. ***A searchlight!***

The General ran back to the square 'I want every soldier dressed and ready to move out in two minutes. I will shoot any man who is not ready to leave; drunk or not' he bawled to the bewildered soldier.

The young girl hugged the sheet around her body and stared at her younger sister trembling in the corner. They had been brought to the compound last evening. They were raped as soon as they entered the hut they were now in; but the ordeal had only begun. One soldier after another came to take his pleasure.

'Why are you doing this' she asked one 'we are all Muslim are we not?'

He had just laughed at her ignorance and pushed himself harder into her already swollen vagina.

She never spoke after that.

There had been a commotion outside. The men had dashed outside and had not returned.

'Sister! Something is happening' she whispered.

'Why worry sister? They will soon return to abuse us more. Allah has abandoned us'

'I don't think so' she said staring out of the window.

She peeked outside. The compound was empty.

Grabbing her sister, she pulled her outside 'it is our chance to escape. Come we will make for the hills'

'If we are not here when they return our father will be thrashed again you know that' she cried.

'We must try. He will understand'

She had lost all hope. Her innocence had been taken from her. The soldiers were animals and deserved to die.

Her sister hugged her.

She began to cry. The tears streamed down her swollen cheeks.

'We have each other. That's all that matters' she whispered softly.

She was about to pull her away when a door opened in one of the huts. Another door opened. Then another.

One by one the women joined them.

'We will all leave this place together' she told them defiantly.

The General ordered one Jeep to check out the searchlight hovering over the dam. The rest would drop down into the village which by now was well ablaze. The Jeep made its way along the road. Headlights full on.

Khan had reached the square tower and radioed Cogan. The whole area was in darkness as the moon disappeared behind a black cloud. He had no option but to switch on his searchlight.

The Jeeps headlights began as a pinprick in the distance but Khan instinctively knew he would not escape the tower before they were in range to fire on the helicopter.

'Back away Cogan while I deal with our unwelcome visitors' he told him.

'Khan that charge is set. If the dam goes, there's no way I can get to you'

He looked at his wristwatch 'there's still time Cogan. I can't risk them taking you out. Sunita is waiting for you'

'I'm staying partner. You have four minutes then I'm coming in'

Khan had already unpacked the Barret M96. Years of training kicked in. He didn't rush and controlled his breathing. In less than a minute the deadly rifle was assembled and being screwed to its tri-pod. A bullet slammed into the chamber. He adjusted the night scope. The cross-hairs came together. He fired.

The driver of the Jeep was thrown back in his seat by the impact.

He reacted by pushing down hard on the power.   The Jeep hit the dam wall; cartwheeled twice and disappeared over the edge into the dam. It sank. Bubbles the only sign of its' passing. It would not reach the dam bottom.

'Come and get me Cogan. Just drop a rope. I think it's time I left'

Khan grabbed the rope and twisted it around his body. The next second he was dangling in mid-air as the helicopter dragged him away.

He felt; more than saw the explosion deep inside the dam. One minute there was a wall; the next it was collapsing in on itself. The water pored over the breach. The breach widened. The lake began to empty.

CHAPTER 13

EXODUS

Sunita had waited until the last of the villagers disappeared along the path. The man she had first met stood beside her unmoving, but occasionally glancing towards the dam in the distance.

It dawned on her he was contemplating following the road that wound its way up the hillside.

'It is not possible to follow the road' she told him 'the water will reach you long before you are safe, and besides, we have company' she said referring to the headlights that had suddenly appeared at the top of the hill.

The man clutched his head in despair.

'What will happen to my daughters. I must find them before the African soldiers return to the compound. They will kill them for sure' he moaned.

'If Khan's plan works there will be no more soldiers to abuse your children' she told him then taking his arm 'we need to leave this place!'

Sunita reached the top of the hill without incident and looked down at the village. The houses and animal pens were well ablaze. Thick smoke curled upwards making her cough. A straw bale would erupt sending flaming embers into the air. The heat from the fires could be felt even here.

In between the burning homes the headlights of the soldiers could be seen making their way through the village.

She took one last look before disappearing over the crest of the hill.

THE VILLAGE

The African General was confused. Where had all the villagers disappeared to. 'Someone is going to pay for this' he snarled kicking a cooking pot into the air.

Every hut was ablaze. The smoke obscured the view; especially from the dam in the distance. Some instinct made him turn around. Light from the burning huts lit up the valley. Something was wrong but what was it? The ground rumbled under his feet. He looked up again; to see the **cascade of water** rushing towards him. The rush of air hit him first throwing him to the ground. He staggered to his feet and threw his cane defiantly at the wall of water. It picked him up like a matchstick in a gutter and swept him away. The water boiled and thrashed down the valley taking everything with it.

The Uranium Mine was next in its path. Cranes and derricks collapsed. Ore trucks tumbled over. A bulldozer defied the impertinence until the ground beneath it collapsed into a shaft below. One by one the other shafts sucked in water; like a thirsty man at a bar. It would not be a viable mine again for many years to come.

The water in the dam drained away. The once sturdy and secure embankment slowly began to crumble. Large chunks of land containing shrubs and boulders slid majestically into the clogging mud of the empty lake.

The re-enforced concrete base of the soldier's compound gave up trying to support the buildings above; as the foundations below crumbled. A large crack appeared. It grew wider by the second splitting the compound into two parts. The block nearest the lake toppled sideways sending vehicles and buildings alike into the darkness below. The building that contained the Uranium processing plant erupted in flames after a large gas cylinder ruptured and then exploded. A storage tank close by was torn from its support. A power line was ripped from its pole. Sparks **crackled** and **spat** like a fourth of July cracker as it thrashed around in the night air. It was enough to ignite the petroleum pouring out of the ruptured tank. Like an angry **Chinese dragon,** the petrol continued to spray out and pour down the side of the hill setting fire to everything in its way. It settled on the remaining water and spread out. The flames casting a glow around the crumbling walls.

CHAPTER 14
THE ESCAPE

Cogan had landed the helicopter at the agreed site some distance from the dam. Khan had not been able to contact Sunita. There was nothing he could do but wait.

It would be impossible to try and find her in the dark and by early morning the place would be crawling with government troops. The moon had finally made an appearance. He tried to control his emotions but the thought of losing her made him fidgety. The woman had affected him more than he cared to admit.

A man carrying a bamboo pole appeared from the gloom. He was obviously a man of importance judging by his appearance. The man put his hand in the air to stop the flow of people behind. He approached Khan and looked him in the eye. Khan didn't blink or make any comment.

The chief continued to stare then burst into a smile.

'The woman was right to trust you; ***profit of doom***!' he laughed.

'Your people should be safe now the men who enslaved you have perished in the flood. It will be many years before the mines are in production again. Will you stay in this country or try to reach Bangladesh?' he asked.

'There is nothing to keep us here except the bones of our young men who perished in the mines'

'I am sorry I couldn't be here sooner' Khan told him sadly.

The Chief studied the man in front of him. It was obvious the calm exterior was a mask he knew few would ever penetrate. There was pain and anger but there was also forgiveness and hope. This man had single handed rescued his people from tyranny. They would not forget him.

'May Allah, protect you, and keep you safe Mohammed Khan' the Chief declared before moving away to his people.

The sisters had heard rather than witnessed the destruction of the compound as they crested the hill and descended into the valley below. The women following had huddled together in fear never realizing how close they had all come to death.

The sister calmed them all and ushered them along the path they were on. The sister stopped suddenly.

A man appeared from the undergrowth. It was their Chief but what was he doing this far from the village?

A woman followed him, then another; carrying a child in a bundle on her back.

She ran up to him and clutched his hand 'what is happening. Where is our father!' she pleaded in despair.

'Calm yourself child. A Profit has visited our village and set us free. Your father is safe. Wait here and he will come to you'

The sisters did as the Chief suggested and sat down on the top of a large boulder to wait. Men and women from the village passed by. A cry! and wail of joy would suddenly be heard as a mother rushed forward to hug the child she believed lost. The young woman would collapse at her mother's feet sobbing in relief at seeing her family again. The shame of her captivity would take time to heal but she would live.

Sunita followed the man from the village. With every step, he believed he was abandoning his children to their fate. His shame weighed heavy on his shoulders.

The clearing was upon them before he realized. He looked up; unable to believe what he was seeing.

Sat alone on top of a large boulder, silhouetted by the moon; were his daughters.

The two women rushed forward as he sank to his knees giving praise to his god. Tears of joy rolled down his cheeks. He clutched his daughters close and asked for their forgiveness.

'There is nothing to forgive father' they whispered.

Sunita struggled not to cry at the sight. She left them and continued along the path. Five minutes later she came upon the helicopter. Khan was pacing back and forth trying to stay calm.

She watched him for a minute before making her appearance.

'**_SUNITA!_**' Khan shouted; making no attempt at keeping the relief from his voice.

Sunita approached him and shook the debris from her hair. She casually smoothed down her tunic and stood erect.

'I do hope you are going to keep your **promise** Michael Khan!'

It took a second for him to understand what she was talking about but when he did he pulled her close and kissed her.

CHAPTER 15
ESCAPE

Cogan had tried arguing; threatening and then pleading but to no avail.

Khan was adamant 'we cannot risk the authorities catching us in your helicopter Cogan you know that. Your CIA cover would be blown for sure and I'm in enough trouble with them as it is'

'But what you are planning to do is madness. You could end up **anywhere**!'

'I've double checked the weather. The wind is favorable and the direction should keep constant for the next few days at least. After that we should be out of the country'

He had given up and said his goodbyes. It was madness but it made sense.

The Airways had been talking about the **terrorist** attack nonstop ever since they left the villagers; who were now well on their way to neighboring Bangladesh.

Sunita sat on a large boulder and crossed her arms defiantly 'if you think I'm going up in that **thing** you are very much mistaken' she told him.

The **thing** was a hot air balloon. Now fully inflated and ready to depart.

'Come on Sunita you'll love it I promise' he said suddenly hauling her over his shoulder and dumping her in the basket. Khan slipped the rope. By the time, she staggered to her feet; the balloon was already soaring into the air.

'You told me you had a secure escape plan. An **Insurance** policy you called it not a **suicide** attempt'

Khan pulled her toward him and kissed her passionately.

'Oh well! Up! Up! and away I suppose' she sighed pulling him down into the basket.

LANGLEY

Head of Operations Director John Cohen welcomed Katherine into his office.

'How is our latest recruit getting on' he asked; indicating her to take a seat.

'She is under **Protective Care** Director Cohen' she replied.

Katherine would omit to say; the protective care was in the form of Michael Khan in a balloon's basket.

The Director noted the formal title 'is there something wrong Kathy'

'How **well** do you know Ex-Director Wyden Sir?'

'I've known him since Law School. We play golf together sometimes' he replied now sensing the tense atmosphere.

'When was the last time you spoke to him?'

'Not since he announced his resignation. What's going on Kathy' he asked again.

'Why was Myanmar not a sanctioned CIA Operation?'

Cohen pushed away the files on his desk 'You know why. Wyden didn't want the Defense Department interfering. His step-daughters' life was at stake. It was only supposed to be a fact-finding trip for that Professor. I thought the Myanmar thing was over'

'Michael Khan had other ideas' she said not wanting to go into details.

The Director leaned forward 'my god! He didn't have anything to do with that dam collapsing, did he?'

She blanked the question for now.

'You received the autopsy on the Professors death. It wasn't an accident like the coroner reported. He was murdered. The file Wyden gave us did not mention the Professor was a leading authority on mining; for **Uranium**!'

'I didn't know. Are you saying that's what he was there for? If that's the case; Wyden must have known. He was the one who recruited him for the mission'

The implication of that statement sunk him. He sat back in his chair.

'It also means I'm guilty by association. I had no idea Kathy but that's no excuse is it. We are in the Spy business. I should have double checked the information'

'You tried to help a friend Director that's all. I almost did the same recently' she said remembering Khans' enquiry 'and it nearly cost me my position here'

She placed a cell phone on the desk and pressed play.

The Director listened to the conversation in the restaurant between Wyden and Sunita.

There was nothing to say. He had made a mistake that's all there was to it.

'I suppose there are two agents in the outer office waiting to escort me to Internal Affairs'

Katherine couldn't meet his eyes 'I'm sorry. I had no choice you know that!'

'Don't be. You are only doing your job' he sighed.

'There is one thing you can help me with before you leave' she said.

'Just ask it!'

'Khan and Sunita are in trouble. I can't explain how or why but if no-one can reach them in the next few hours they may die'

'What can I do?'

'You mentioned a few days ago; about a **Nuclear Submarine**?'

He made a call.

BAY OF BENGAL

Khan checked again the GPS reckoning. He had made a mistake and it could cost them their lives. The low altitude slip-stream had pushed them further south than expected. He could have landed the balloon before moving out to sea but that would have meant putting down in Myanmar.

He had gambled the warm air current from off the ocean would push them back towards the coast of Bangladesh. It didn't. They were now past the point of no-return. He gazed down at the placid sea below. It looked calm and inviting. It was deceptive. The gas cylinder was almost empty. The balloon above was already deflating. They would soon have to ditch in the sea. They had life jackets but exiting a balloon was dangerous on dry land. At sea, the risks multiplied.

'If we get caught under the canopy as the balloon deflates we could be dragged down when it sinks' he told Sunita.

His last contact with Katherine had been over two hours ago, the signal had been lost after that.

Khan gently shook Sunita awake 'we have to get ready. I'm sorry for putting you in danger like this' he said.

She pulled him down and kissed him 'we're in this together Michael'

It was no good waiting. They were only drifting further out to sea. Khan made sure Sunita had secured the life jacket.

'When I say **now**! Jump as far away from the basket as you can; then swim away from the balloon. We can't take anything with us. You understand?'

She nodded then frowned. She then pointed down.

'What is **that**' she said as the sea erupted below them.

Khan looked down and began laughing **'it's our ride home'** he said hugging her.

EPILOGUE

CENTRAL PARK NEW YORK

Michael moved his Queen across the board and received a *'Hum'* from the man opposite.

His opponent scratched his head for a few moments then tipped his King over in defeat 'you are getting quite a reputation Michael, and I'm not just talking about your chess game' he smiled glancing across at the woman sitting on a bench close by.

Sunita was chatting away happily to his father.

They had got on like a house on fire ever since they met.

She had insisted on meeting him as soon as they returned from their mission in Myanmar. Sunita was independent, clever and resourceful. She also spoke more languages than he had even heard of.

She was also a woman in love.

Meeting his father was her way of stating her intentions. Khan had no objections in that direction but marriage and a family were not a consideration. At least in the near future. The memory of his wife and son killed in a village in Africa was still too raw.

'I will let another player sit down' his opponent said standing up.

'I think someone wants to join me Judge and he doesn't look like a chess player to me?'

The Judge in question raised an eyebrow *'trouble?'* he asked concerned for the son of his old friend.

'I don't think so Sir but if it is its nothing I can't handle'

The Judge wasn't going to argue with that. Michael or Mohammed Khan as he was also known as was a highly-trained Army Officer and CIA Agent.

The man in question decided it was the right time to approach his prey. He walked casually across the triangle and was about to say something when Khan interrupted.

'Can you play chess or do you just wish to talk!' he asked before he even opened his mouth.

The man was taken aback for a moment; then understood he had already been spotted lurking in the distance 'my apologies Mr. Khan. Your reputation precedes you. My attempt at subterfuge was silly given your background'

Khan studied the man as he sat down. He was middle-aged but physically very fit. He assumed an air of self-confidence even importance. He was well dressed. The suit was not purchased in a ready to wear men's store.

The man waited understanding he was being scrutinised.

'You do not have a military background so I'm ruling out the armed forces. Possibly FBI or CIA but I suspect even those two bad arses would be too mundane for a man of your background and intelligence. Are you a Civil Servant? Possibly from some unknown State Department we will never hear of?'

The man nodded 'close enough Mr. Khan. My name is Theodore Kingsley' he said offering his hand in welcome.

'How can I help you Mr. Kingsley'

'The answer to your first question is yes! I do play chess. White to move' he said pushing a Pawn forward 'although I confess I haven't played since Princeton'

'Do I detect a slight British accent as well' Khan asked.

'Grandmother came from Oxford in England. She insisted I get a *proper* education and packed me off to Cambridge for two years. She's related to Royalty you know' he said proudly.

They played chess. Kingsley was good despite his lack of game practice.

It ended in a draw. They shook hands.

'We need your help Mr. Khan' Kingsley stated.

'Why not ask the CIA. I am under Contract to them'

'Something which can be annulled by a telephone call I assure you. However, it is not under your *given* name that I wish to employ you'

Khan was impressed by the first statement but confused and wary about the second.

'You have me at a disadvantage Mr. Kingsley' he asked probing.

Kingsley looked him in the eye 'I do not have the luxury or the time to play games Mr. Khan so I will now dispense with the verbal foreplay and lay my cards on the table. When I have finished, all I require is a yes or no answer'

Khan nodded.

'Twenty-four hours ago, a commercial cruise ship was hi-jacked off the coast of South Africa. On board are one hundred children between the ages of fifteen and eighteen. We can only estimate the number of crew and other adults still on board including any security agents providing protection for the children. The Hijackers have demanded a ransom of three hundred million dollars by transfer to a bank in Panama. Diamonds and other precious gems to a value of three hundred million US dollars! A shopping list of weapons has also been provided. This list includes Surface to Air missiles'

Khan was genuinely taken aback but he quickly recovered 'there has been nothing on the news about this'

'Not yet Mr. Khan but that is about to change. I don't even know how we have kept this under wraps for this long to be honest'

'Who are *we*?'

'**We** are a department attached to the United Nations Security Council! We have the backing of all the main UN Members and their full support to do whatever is necessary. We do not answer to any one Nation rather the

UN itself. It was established for an event such as this'

'My experience with the UN has not been a good one Mr. Kingsley; as you may know. But you still haven't answered my second question'

'We wish to hire Mister Suleiman. Internationally renowned purchaser of Jewels and rare Artefacts'

Michael couldn't help the surprise coming on his face.

Kingsley smiled aware he had finally shaken the reserved composure from the man opposite.

This was not the time to play games however 'your name, or should I say Mister Suleiman's name was on a list provided by the Hijackers. The diamonds and precious jewels have been split between three different Brokers. One is in Amsterdam. One is in Hong Kong and one in New York'

'A clever ploy by the Hijackers' Khan decided 'that many diamonds and other jewels collected in one place would never be a secret for long. How did Suleiman's name come to be on the list?'

'A good question and one my Agency have been struggling with since we received it. You see you don't exist do you. We contacted every US Agencies including Home Security. It was only by chance some bright young woman at the CIA saw the MEMO and called us'

Khan suspected who that was. The mission to rescue the people in Myanmar had not been officially sanctioned. The names and the details had been kept between the few people around the table at his first meeting in the CIA Headquarters. Not even the soon to be disgraced Ex-Director knew about the fake buyer of precious jewels called Suleiman.

It was now becoming clear why the UN Agency wanted to hire him.

'How much did Miss Carter tell you about me?'

'I have just left the young woman in question' he answered trying to move on as fast as possible to a conclusion 'when I explained what had happened she was more than willing to co-operate. Like I said; time is of the essence Mister Khan'

'The persona of Mister Suleiman is still valid. I did my best not to blow his cover but I never believed I would have to re-invent him so soon'

'Whatever you did in Egypt and Myanmar has convinced the Organisation responsible for the kidnapping to trust you or at least you can be trusted to break the rules to suit your needs. I must say I am impressed. Not many fake backgrounds pass the test of close scrutiny'

'Are you saying the ransom is to be paid? Given most countries stance on that subject I would think that could be a problem even with children involved'

'I would agree, and the UN has the same edict. But we are talking about children from a dozen different countries. The children are the sons and daughters of wealthy and influential People. They have already made their thoughts known. The ransom is too paid wherever possible. Money is not the issue here'

'What about the arms. Will the US agree to pass over their latest Defence Missiles?'

Kingston went quiet as he considered what to do next.

He looked Khan in the eye 'there is much I haven't disclosed and will not do so unless I have your answer' he stated bluntly.

Khan studied the man from the UN. He was being asked to get involved in something that could have serious political repercussions not to mention the security consequences. The Kidnappers where being very clever in their demands. But how had this been allowed to happen in the first place he thought.

'I will do whatever is necessary to help you Mister Kingston. On condition you reveal everything that has happened so far. You know who I am and what I can achieve. Paying the ransom is only part of this. What you really need is a way to rescue the children; *unharmed*. If you say the children are from different countries, then I can assume plans have been put forward for a rescue'

'There are many plans, but they have already been discounted as unpractical or dangerous. There is something you should know. It will be on every news channel in exactly two hours anyway. I have already said the children are from different countries but some were released immediately'

'You mean they weren't on the ship?'

'They *were* on the cruise ship when it left Johannesburg but the Russian and Chinese children were not taken. They left them on the Island before leaving'

Khan processed the information 'whoever is organising this is very clever as I have already said. By not taking certain children they are splitting the other countries opinion and breaking a possible united front. The fact they are Chinese and Russian will only fuel the suspicions of other countries. They may even think they had been complicit in it all'

'An opinion I have already come to Mister Khan. The political fallout here could be terrible. I know that sounds callous but it is something I must consider'

'Who else knows you are here Kingston'

'My Director and your Miss Carter of course' he added.

'Good! Let's keep it that way. I work better alone, but I will need Miss Carter as my liaison and back-up'

'You will have anything you need but I must approve any rescue plan. I will have Miss Carter transferred to our Command Centre near to the UN Building. I have one more person to visit then I will be there myself. Here is the address' he said handing over instructions.

Khan noted the address and then ripped the card to pieces 'old habits die hard' he said smiling 'I will be there in one hour'

Kingston held out his hand 'I'm placing a lot of trust in your abilities Khan but I have a feeling it is well founded'

Kingston walked away briskly. One of his agents appeared from nearby and escorted him to a waiting car.

Khan watched them depart and frowned.

The reference to diamonds had him thinking back on the recent events in Myanmar.

'Could this kidnapping be linked somehow?' he thought.

'What was that all about?' Sunita asked as she joined him.

'I have to leave. Do you mind if Dad gives you a ride home' he said trying to sound casual.

She looked at him 'that wasn't a passing question Michael. Please give me credit for knowing there **is** a problem' she said stubbornly.

He smiled 'I should know better than to fool you but there is no time now. Will you trust me when I say it's important I leave straight away?'

Sunita tapped the screen on the cell phone she was holding 'does it have anything to do with **this**?' she asked.

Michael looked and shook his head 'I think it was wishful thinking on Kingston's part to believe they would hold the story back'

'So I'm right. The man from the UN has asked for your help!'

'It seems I have a reputation for getting people out of sticky situations'

'I'm coming with you' she declared 'and before you start to argue; let me ask you this.

236

Those children are from different countries. Do you think all of them speak English?'

Michael sighed in resignation.

She was right and he knew it. Her skills as a Linguist would be invaluable.

He held out his arm 'come on **Partner**! **Let's go and sink a ship**!'

'I assume by that statement you already have a **plan in mind'** she grinned happily.

TO BE CONTINUED.

ABOUT THE AUTHOR
Michael Johnson was born in Yorkshire; England, but has lived in Southern Spain for many years. His writing career began late in life after meeting published authors and deciding it was time to start that novel! His first book was published one year later.

Other Novels by the author.
Mike Johnson
The David Fallon Detective Series
Dragon
The Korean Connection
The Buddha in Ice
The Bankers
Stealth

Short Stories
Stories from the Bar

ALL AVAILABLE TO DOWNLOAD

Table of Contents

www.ingramcontent.com/pod-product-compliance
Lightning Source LLC
Chambersburg PA
CBHW070456200726
48293CB00007B/2225